MAKE FRIENDS

WITH

MURDER

MAKE FRIENDS WITH MURDER

Judith Garwood

ST. MARTIN'S PRESS   NEW YORK

MAKE FRIENDS WITH MURDER. Copyright © 1992 by Judith Garwood. All
rights reserved. Printed in the United States of America. No part of this
book may be used or reproduced in any manner whatsoever without
written permission except in the case of brief quotations embodied in
critical articles or reviews. For information, address St. Martin's Press, 175
Fifth Avenue, New York, N.Y. 10010.

Design by Judith Dannecker

Library of Congress Cataloging-in-Publication Data

Garwood, Judith.
    Make friends with murder / Judith Garwood.
        p.   cm.
    "A Thomas Dunne book."
    ISBN 0-312-07030-6
    I. Title.
    PS3557.A8424M35   1992
    813'.54—dc20   91-33421
                                                                                    CIP

First Edition: February 1992

10 9 8 7 6 5 4 3 2 1

Grateful acknowledgment is made for permission to reprint an excerpt
from "Sonnet XXX" of *Fatal Interview* by Edna St. Vincent Millay. From
Collected Poems, Harper & Row. Copyright © 1931, 1958 by Edna St.
Vincent Millay and Norma Millay Ellis. Reprinted by permission of Eliza-
beth Barnett, literary executor.

FOR WB
who said why don't you stop reading those damn things
and write one

I would like to thank Les Roberts, who liked this book before anyone else; Phyllis Brown, who encouraged me when I needed it most; my editor Ruth Cavin and my agent Maureen Lasher, who each gave me a second chance.

Love can not fill the thickened lung with breath,
Nor clean the blood, nor set the fractured bone;
Yet many a man is making friends with death
Even as I speak, for lack of love alone.

—Edna St. Vincent Millay

MAKE FRIENDS
WITH
MURDER

1

I left for Santa Clarissa about the middle of the afternoon. Everything for the picnic was done except for the fruit. We could pick up some bread at a local bakery. I had thought about baking the bread myself, but you only do that at the beginning of the relationship, when you want to impress somebody. Besides, it was too hot.

I kissed the cats goodbye, reassured them that Norman would come over in the morning to feed them, put the top down on my Alfa Romeo Spider, stuffed my hair into a cap, and headed north.

Once out of L.A. and into the foothills, brown and dry to the point of cracking with late summer drought, I started looking forward to the week.

I was glad I had waited until Monday. There was construction on the highway near Camarillo (there was always construction on the highway near Camarillo), the road was down to only two lanes, and if I had been facing weekend traffic, the drive would have been interminable. I was wearing only a gray silk camisole and jeans, and two hours was just enough sun and wind. Any more and I would burn, despite my tan.

Downshifting for the construction made me acutely aware of how stiff my legs were. I had taken a self-defense workshop on Saturday and almost settled into premature middle age afterward. I didn't want to think it might not be that premature. Six hours of hitting pillows, aiming for imaginary eyes, ears, and noses, squeezing the balls and crushing the knee-caps of a straw man named Ralph the Rapist, breaking the chokeholds and bear hugs of a partner, and having one's chokeholds and bear hugs broken in return had left me both exhilarated and exhausted.

"Don't be *compliant*," the instructor, a short, heavyset young woman with a firm jaw, and a long dark braid wrapped around her head, had yelled at us. "*Fight back!* Do you want to get hurt?"

"No," we had murmured raggedly, uneasily.

"Louder!" the instructor had shouted.

The noise from the group had been a little stronger.

"Let me hear it LOUDER! NO! NO!" The instructor had led us, as if it were a chant.

We began chanting with her. "NO! NO! NO! NO!" We were not compliant, and we would learn not to be hurt, if possible. We all wanted to learn how to keep from getting hurt. Or getting hurt again.

After the workshop, I had driven painfully back to my house—a small blue Spanish-style bungalow in the Silver Lake area of Los Angeles—in a state so close to total depletion that I was shivering, even in the ninety-degree heat that had settled in several days earlier, turning the basin into a frying pan.

I had been so tired that it was all I could do to feed the cats and call Tom to tell him I couldn't drive up on Sunday after all, it would have to be Monday. I had promised him a picnic on Tuesday. Wednesday I would have to start interviews. I was partly looking forward to seeing him. I was looking forward even more to researching the article on the Santa Clarissa Valley wineries for *Explore!* magazine.

Hitting another ridge, seeing another valley ahead, with its scattering of sumac and live oak trees, made me think of what the country must have been like when the first Californios rode up from Mexico. I had what felt like a racial memory of riding over that same ridge on horseback and seeing the valley, with no houses, and knowing that I would settle here forever. I began to regain my normal feeling of eternal youth.

Driving through Santa Barbara I had to downshift again. I could never understand why someone hadn't insisted that a freeway be built around the town. Santa Barbarans couldn't possibly love that bottleneck. It was always rush hour in Santa Barbara. Or never rush hour, depending on your perspective, because it never got any better, but it never got any worse.

One stoplight changed three times before I finally got to the intersection. I happened to glance up at the light for the cross street, on the corner to my right, and was momentarily unnerved by what appeared to be a face looking back at me. Looking again, I realized that it was a doll's head. Someone had placed a severed baby doll's head in the niche where the green light shone. I drove on feeling a little less joy in the day.

Past Santa Barbara, I made the turn toward Lake Cachuma and reached Tom's house while the day was still hot and bright.

He came to the door, naked except for a pair of khaki shorts, as I pulled up in the dirt driveway. Once his body would have stopped my heart. He had gained a little weight since leaving the police department, but his muscles were still well defined, thanks to a set of weights in the house and what were probably daily workouts.

His hair was longer now, curling around the back of his neck. His dark mustache was shaggy, and he hadn't shaved in a day or so. He would have looked handsomer if he hadn't been scowling.

"It's about time," he said.

I shook my hair loose from the cap, which I stuck in the glove compartment.

"How about, 'Hey, it's really good to see you'?" I said, not moving.

"Yeah, okay, it's really good to see you."

I got out of the car as he moved toward me. I started to kiss him lightly on the lips, but he didn't disengage. And I decided maybe I was glad to see him after all.

"I'm hot and sweaty," I murmured.

"I know you are," he whispered. "So am I."

He embraced me gently, and I allowed myself to relax, my head in the hollow of his neck and shoulder, breathing in his muskiness. Like a cat, I've always relied on scent to recognize a man as my lover. He leaned down and kissed me again.

We unpacked the car about an hour later.

When we had both showered and dried, and once my things and the picnic stuff for the next day were put away, he poured us each a glass of wine and sat down on the big leather sofa across from the unlit fireplace. He had furnished the house in a heavy Spanish style, with a lot of dark oak. But he hadn't overdone it. The effect was real Old West ranch house.

"So how was your self-defense workshop?" Tom asked. Politely, dutifully.

"It was great. I really have a whole different sense of taking care of myself. Walking into the grocery store feels different. And I'm sleeping better at night."

"Come on. You slept better for two nights because you were tired. You don't get all that much from one day."

"Yeah, I got all that much from one day. Believe me, it was a long day."

He looked at me skeptically. "Don't get overconfident."

I bristled. "Try something," I said.

He looked at me and shook his head. "Let's not play that game."

"You started it," I replied, setting my wine glass on the carved end table. "Try something."

He reached over and set his wine glass next to mine.

4

Abruptly, he grabbed my wrists and pushed me back onto the couch, pinning me down. "Now what?"

I planted my heels firmly, thrust sharply with my pelvis, and stuck my right arm out. He was now on the floor next to the couch. I was on top.

"Notice where my knee is," I said.

He breathed in sharply. "Okay. I wasn't expecting that. You did learn a lot in one day." He let go of my wrists.

"You don't sound pleased."

I wasn't feeling very pleased myself. Not as pleased as I had wanted to feel. The self-defense instructor had warned us not to test our ability on people we loved, that we shouldn't take the chance of hurting someone we loved. I had just taken that chance. I sort of slid back up onto the couch. Tom got up stiffly.

"I'm glad you feel you can take care of yourself, because I know that's important to you. I know how upset you were when you were in danger and couldn't do anything about it. But I'm afraid you're going to get into trouble. Sometimes your ego is stronger than your judgment."

"That's a bunch of shit. That sounds like something my father would have said."

"Your father would have been right, too. And I still wish you'd let me teach you how to use a gun."

"I don't want a gun. Guns kill people." I wished I could take that back. If he hadn't killed someone with a gun, I would have been dead. "I'm sorry. I don't want to have this argument right now."

"What do you want to do?"

"Since I'm here, I want us to hold each other for a while. Then maybe we should think about dinner or something."

"Okay." He sat down beside me, holding his arms out.

I lost myself again in the warmth of his body. There were moments when I thought it would be nice to let go permanently, to stay here, to drowse through the rest of my life like this. But they always passed.

The sky was turning pink by the time we managed to get

ourselves together enough to think about dinner. One of the things I liked about Tom was that he always let me take my time, he never asked me to hurry up so we could get someplace. I was relieved, finding something I liked about him. I did like him. I just—really—wasn't sure I loved him.

We drove down to Los Robles in Tom's black Porsche, still with the CPWRITR license plate. I had asked him if he missed being a cop, and he had said no, but I wondered if he meant it. He had to be lonely here—the loneliness of the long-distance writer. He had told me that I was the only thing he missed about Los Angeles. I couldn't believe that.

Los Robles, a sleepy little tourist attraction about ten minutes away, comprised an assortment of art galleries and wineries and not much else. The hotel was improbably large and improbably Victorian. Also improbably expensive. But then the food was improbably good. The gallery owners and the winemakers and the owners of the nearby Arabian ranches evidently did quite well. Or they had done quite well at something else (as Tom had) before they moved here.

I ordered a salad of watercress and pine nuts and the poached salmon with champagne sorrel sauce. Tom ordered a spinach salad with a warm bacon dressing and filet mignon with raspberry sauce. I winced as he ordered red meat.

One of the things that had gone wrong in our relationship was that he had held back any opinions that were different from mine while we were first getting to know each other. Avoiding confrontations was okay—although I tend not to— but he had gone too far. Now, as his true feelings came out, I found that I was trusting him less. I didn't feel as if I had the security to tell secrets—I felt as if he had misled me before. And not just about red meat. Red meat was dumb. But other things were important. (Like what? Like how much he needed a relationship, maybe. And one with a more traditional woman, or at least one who was willing to play a more traditional role.) So I found myself increasingly irritated with him, except when we were in bed together.

We ordered two half bottles of wine, a Cabernet and a

6

Chardonnay. The Chardonnay, from one of the wineries on my list, was better than I had expected. I looked at the label, a reproduction of a painting of a bunch of grapes. The original was probably a watercolor. Novelli Winery. Novelli was going to be my first interview Wednesday morning.

As the waiter arrived with our salads, I realized that I had been silent for a while, and that Tom had been looking at me.

"What?" I asked.

"I'm the one who should ask that," he replied.

I shrugged. "Actually, I was thinking about the wine. When Fred asked me to come up here and do a story on the Santa Clarissa wineries, I wasn't aware they had anything this good."

"I thought you weren't going to talk about your work tonight."

"Well, you wanted to know what I was thinking about. And I was thinking about my work. And I don't understand why you resent that."

"And I don't understand why you write this magazine crap. You're a better writer than that."

One reason he didn't like to confront me is that I don't always react well. I thought before answering. " 'This magazine crap' is how I make a living," was all I said.

That reminded me of one more thing that wasn't working about the relationship. I didn't want him to know I was working on a novel. I didn't want to show it to him, didn't want his opinion of it. Not because I didn't admire his work. Just because I didn't want to know what he thought of mine. Nothing he said about it could make things easier between us, and if he tried to make suggestions—if I felt he was trying to control my work, the way I sometimes felt he wanted to control my life—it would only make things worse.

"It sounds like you're saying that's why you're here."

"Well, it is."

Tom was silent for a minute, his face tight. He rubbed his forehead with one of his large hands. "I shouldn't have pushed you into that. I'm sorry. But this isn't working, Morgan. I don't like having you with me part-time, when you feel like it."

"I know. You've said that before. And I've told you before—I told you when you moved up here—that I'm not sure I want to tear up my life for you."

"Why don't you stay for a while, see how you feel?"

"Because my four cats, my peahen, and my word processor are all in Los Angeles. You'd keep working, but there would be no place for me to work. And I guess because I don't think I want to stay."

"What do you want?"

"I don't know," I answered, feeling a rising sense of panic. "I guess I've just never been very good at sustaining intimate relationships, and it doesn't look as if I'm going to start now."

"What does that mean?"

"It means that I'm already as close to you as I want to get. Maybe closer."

"Are you saying you want to end it?"

"I'm not sure. I'm saying I'm not comfortable with it, and I'm not sure why. You're offering me a lot of things I feel I should want, and I can't figure out why I feel terrified at the thought of accepting them. But I do. Something deep inside me suspects that any close relationship with a man is ultimately an oppressive relationship. And when I'm with you, I sometimes start feeling as if you take me over—not intentionally, it's just the way you are—and I want to go home."

"Is that what you want now?"

"If we're not careful, we're going to ruin a good dinner, and I hate that."

"What do you want to do?" His voice was sharp.

"I don't want to be pushed—you know I hate to be pushed."

"I know. But this is more important than what time we eat."

I searched for something we could both live with. Maybe I'm not as good at confrontations as I like to think.

"Okay. I want to stay tonight and have a picnic and tour the

8

wineries with you tomorrow. And I won't take notes. After that, I don't know. I'm not sure it's a good idea for me to use your house as a base while I interview owners and winemakers."

We had agreed that I would. I watched him carefully as I backed out, and I still barely caught the flicker of vulnerability.

"Look—" He stopped himself.

I couldn't stand the silence. "Why don't we talk about something noncontroversial like the situation in the Mideast?"

"I could do without your bad jokes," he said.

"Well, I guess you won't miss me when I leave tomorrow, then." I was stung and blurted it out.

After that, there wasn't much to say.

And later, something happened that had never happened before, that I hadn't anticipated, that let me know how hurt he was: we went to bed in silence and didn't make love.

I didn't sleep well, and I didn't think he did either, although I didn't ask. He was up early, and I could hear him in the bathroom, then in the kitchen, starting coffee. Staying even for the picnic started to seem like a bad idea. I thought about getting up and getting dressed and leaving. I felt small and unbearably lonely, lying by myself in his big bed. I was dwarfed by the heavy Spanish furniture, the dark wardrobe and dresser, by the disorder of his life spread out for me to see, keys and coins and jeans and socks. How could he work with so much in disarray around him? I needed things neat, even if there was dust in the corners. Maybe he couldn't work. We hadn't even talked about how his new book was going.

The morning light was getting stronger, falling softly through the woven curtains, making patterns on the old-fashioned hooked blue area rugs. I did covet those rugs and the hardwood floors. I wondered if I would ever wake up in that bedroom again.

I couldn't hear him in the kitchen any longer, and I wondered what he was doing. I thought again about getting up, but I didn't know what I would say to him. Then I heard him coming up the stairs to the bedroom.

Our eyes met as he walked through the door. I couldn't read his expression.

"I thought you might want coffee," he said, holding out a speckled pottery mug with an ivy leaf pattern.

I had given him the mugs as a housewarming present.

I sat up in bed, holding the pale blue sheet around my body, not wanting to be naked just then. He was wearing only the same khaki shorts he had worn the day before, apparently unconcerned about his own seminakedness.

"Thanks," I said, taking the mug. The coffee was black. That he had forgotten I took cream in my coffee detracted from the gift a little. I sipped it anyway. He made good coffee, and I could drink it black if I had to. But I wanted to make sure I had to. "Is there any cream?"

"Oh, hell, I forgot," he said. "I'm not sure if there is or not. There may be milk, but I don't know if it's any good. I'll check."

He started to leave again.

"That's okay," I said. "I have to get up anyway, and I'll get it."

He sat down on the edge of the bed. The only chair in the room, a rocking chair, held the blue and white patchwork quilt that would cover the bed when it was made. I had folded it neatly and placed it there the night before.

Something was different about him this morning. He smelled different. He didn't smell like my lover any more. He smelled like a stranger. He looked different, too. I could see the pores in his skin, I was conscious of the hair follicles, of the white flakes of dead skin. He seemed to be decomposing in front of me.

"About last night—" He stopped. "How do you feel this morning?"

"I'm okay," I lied. "How are you?"

"Okay, I guess."

I knew he wanted to reach out to me.

"I have to go to the bathroom," I said. I slid out of bed on the side away from him, taking the coffee mug with me.

The house was old, and the plumbing wasn't terrific. The pipes were clogged with age, and after flushing the toilet, one had to wait for the tank to refill before running water anywhere else in the house. So I went down to the kitchen to look for cream before trying to take a shower.

The kitchen had been redecorated by the last owner of the house in new wood cabinets, Mexican tile, and modern appliances, including a dishwasher and a microwave, all cheery yellow. The carton of half-and-half in the cheery yellow refrigerator was clearly, from the date on it, left over from my last visit. I threw it out without smelling it. I fared a little better with the low-fat milk, although I didn't like the color my coffee turned. Cream made coffee richer; low-fat milk simply diluted it.

Tom showed up as I was putting the carton back in the refrigerator. He was wearing running shoes and socks and a T-shirt.

"What's your schedule?" he asked. He was withdrawn, polite.

"I thought I'd take a shower and wash my hair," I answered uncomfortably. "Then—if you want me to—I'd like to read what you've done on your book. We could talk about it over the picnic."

"Before or after we tour the Novelli Winery?"

I ignored the edge in his voice. "That's up to you—and I guess it depends on how much you have written, and how long I take reading it."

He softened a little. "I'll leave the manuscript in the living room for you. I want to run. I'll probably be back in about an hour, and we'll see where you are then."

"You're going to run for an hour? Are you in training for a marathon all of a sudden?"

"No, I just feel like running this morning."

"Okay. I'll see you when you get back."

He seemed to want to say something more, but he didn't. He turned and headed out the kitchen door. Through the window, I could see him starting to run down the drive toward the road.

I showered, dried myself with one of his dark green oversize towels, pulled on jeans and a Mexican cotton shirt, and curled up on the leather sofa to read the manuscript Tom had left for me. It was maybe a hundred pages, typewritten. I couldn't understand why he didn't buy a word processor.

Before I picked it up, I sat for a moment, looking out the picture window. The house was above the road. There were trees planted close, which gave privacy. Beyond, there were fields, some with high-wired grapevines, bright green against the surrounding brown hillsides. I wondered who they belonged to, what kind of grapes, what kind of wine. I was looking forward more and more to doing the article.

I picked up the manuscript.

I heard him come back from his run, but he didn't come into the living room. I heard him in the shower, then nothing, then the typewriter in the room where he worked. Evidently he was going to work while I read. I didn't interrupt him until I was ready to leave for the winery, the picnic packed.

I rapped on the door frame to let him know I was there, walked over to him, kissed him lightly on the neck, and put the manuscript down on the massive oak desk next to his IBM Selectric. It was a good room to work in. Like the living room, it had a large window facing the fields and vineyards to the south.

"You've got some good stuff here," I said.

He swiveled around in the heavy leather chair to face me. He had changed into clean khaki shorts and a Mexican cotton shirt much like mine.

"Thanks," he said, and he sounded as if he cared that I liked it.

I was touched by him for a moment, touched that he was vulnerable where I was concerned. "I can find something else to do if you'd like to work a while longer."

12

"No, let's go."

The day was warm and dry as we stepped out into it. Tom strapped the ice chest onto the back of the Harley and handed me a helmet. I pinned my hair so that it wouldn't blow, adjusted the helmet, and straddled the Harley behind him. I grabbed the waistband of his shorts as he suddenly started the engine, and leaned into the curve with him as he turned from the driveway onto the road.

The Novelli Winery was just the other side of Santa Clarissa. Although the Novellis had a relatively small output— only about twelve thousand cases a year—they had a large promotion budget. Virtually all of the wine was sold to the visitors who toured the winery, either on the spot or through the quarterly newsletter sent to everyone who signed the guest book. I had found out that much about them before leaving Los Angeles.

I also knew that they were the first in the valley to plant Pinot Noir grapes, and that since the Santa Clarissa Valley appeared to be better suited to these grapes than anywhere else in California, the winery had a head start in what might be an important wine. They had not only won the usual local gold medals, which almost every California winery displayed, but also gained recognition in a couple of international tastings. They boasted about the care they took with their grapes. It would be a few more years before anyone really knew how the vines would mature and how the wines would age, but the smart money was betting on the Novellis. A friend of mine who knew a lot more about wine than I did had bought a case of the 1987 vintage to join the case of 1984 that he had already put away.

My first impression as Tom slowed the bike and slid gracefully into a space in the almost empty parking lot was that this wasn't really a winery—it was a movie set, made up to look like a winery. In the bright morning sun the stucco was too white, the tiles were too red, the surrounding vines were too green. At any moment the huge wooden doors were going to swing open and Zorro himself, in his Don Diego guise, was

13

going to hold his arms out to us and say, *"Mi casa, su casa."* It didn't happen.

Instead, we fussed a little and decided that the ice chest was safe on the bike while we toured and tasted. And when we walked up to those dark, ornately carved doors, the spell was broken. There was a large sign to the left of the doors announcing the identity of the winery, the hours the gift shop was open, and the times of the tours. The doors themselves had been marred by a sign above one large polished knob that said Pull.

Tom pulled, and we found ourselves in a gift shop. Again, it was a movie-set gift shop, even to the sawdust on the floor. Immediately in front of us was a rack of T-shirts. One displayed prominently bore the legend "Life is too short to drink bad wine."

I checked the price tag. It wasn't cheap.

To our left was a rack of books on wine and the California wine industry, including cookbooks. Beyond, there were displays of mustards and vinegars and corkscrews and various shiny utensils labeled Wine Accessories. To our right was a small bar with a very young woman in a plaid shirt and jeans behind it. She had a bright, pretty face and long dark hair partly covered with a cotton scarf.

"Hi," she said, with the unforced cheer that only very young women have. "The tour is just leaving, but you can catch it. We'll start a tasting at the end of the tour."

She pointed past the bar to the right, where we could see a small knot of people.

I glanced at Tom. We both shrugged and wandered toward the group.

Another very young woman, who looked as if she might be a sister to the one behind the bar, was leading the group out a side door toward the vineyard.

"Taste the grapes," she was saying as we caught up. "You'll be amazed at how sweet they are."

The grapes were tiny and very green. I was indeed amazed at how sweet they were.

14

"What kind of grapes are they?" I whispered to the tall, fleshy, polyester-clad woman next to me, who was also tasting a grape.

"Chardonnay," the woman whispered back.

The guide continued her spiel as we passed metal troughs and tanks and peered into rooms with oak barrels of various sizes. I caught some of it, including the dig at other wineries for using their barrels too long. But I had decided that this trip was just for atmosphere, and that I would keep my word to Tom not to take notes.

"Through these doors are the Novelli wine cellars," the guide announced pretentiously as she started to push on one of a pair of heavy oak doors that rivaled those at the front of the building. She seemed a bit disconcerted when the door wouldn't budge. She pushed harder.

"I don't think it's locked," she said uncertainly. "But it is the first tour of the day so I guess it might be." She pushed again. "It feels as if there's something blocking it."

A large, balding man, the companion of the polyester woman, stepped forward and pushed on the door. It gave a few inches.

The man glanced through the door and turned back to the group. "Somebody give me a hand here," he said, with a touch of panic in his voice.

Tom and I both moved forward. As Tom helped push the door open, I could see what was blocking it.

There was a body on the floor of the wine cellar.

2

Tom stepped through the narrow opening, letting the door close behind him with a whoosh of cool air—air that should have been welcome—from the cellar. I turned to the tour guide.

"Why don't you take everyone back to the tasting room?" I suggested.

The young woman nodded and called (too brightly now) to the small group. "Okay, everybody this way. We're going to have to skip the cellars, but wine's better to drink than to look at anyway!"

I slipped through the door and found Tom kneeling beside the body of a man dressed in a gray sweatsuit. The man was prone, partially curled, reaching as if he had been trying to get out the door but hadn't quite made it. I took a deep breath to stay calm, but it was a mistake. I caught a whiff of something that almost triggered my gag reflex. The stench came from a pool of what appeared to be bloody vomit. I walked away for a moment, down the row of wine bottles, to control the flips my stomach was doing.

Coming back, I decided to breathe through my mouth. I got as close as I could, looking over Tom's shoulder. I couldn't see the man's face, only a mop of blond hair, but I had a sense that he was fairly young.

"He's dead," Tom said quietly. He stood between me and the body, pushing me toward the door. "I'll wait with the body. Get somebody to call the police and make sure no one leaves until they get here."

I headed for the tasting room, wondering how I was supposed to make sure no one left when I didn't even know who was here. The only other time I had been close to a dead body, it had been dark, and Tom had grabbed me and pushed me away then, too. Now I was caught between terror, repugnance, and a truly morbid fascination.

The very young woman behind the bar in the gift shop/ tasting room was still smiling, but now it was forced, the cheer was gone. The guide had started back toward the cellar and met me in the doorway.

"Call the police," I said to her quietly. "And tell your friend to keep the wine flowing."

The young woman nodded. "I've already called," she said.

I headed out to the parking lot, where I could spot anyone trying to leave. And I could wait for the police there. I wondered what it was like for Tom, sitting there with a dead body. I knew, sadly, that it wasn't the first time he had done that.

The Santa Clarissa County sheriff's deputies arrived about twenty minutes later. Two couples had tried to leave—the large man and the polyester woman and two slender young men—but in each case they had agreed to stay until the police arrived. None of them questioned my authority.

I introduced myself to the deputies and led them to the wine cellar. Both deputies were young, the older of the two perhaps in his midthirties. He was also the taller of the two, even a couple of inches taller than Tom, who touched six feet, and he already had that slightly beefy ex-jock look. He had a

17

small scar on his left cheekbone, the kind you see on boxers. His black hair curled over the edges of his ears. It wasn't as long as Tom's, but it seemed a little too long for a cop.

His partner looked sweaty and uncomfortable, as if this were the first time he had seen a dead body. His face was white, his light brown hair clinging limply around it.

The first deputy introduced himself as Will Baca, his partner as Jerry Harris. When Tom gave his name, Baca held out his hand and said, "Good to meet you. I've read your books." Tom merely nodded, and Baca knelt down to look at the body. He muttered something to Harris, who left, obviously relieved. "What happened, Francesca?" he asked without looking up.

Francesca (Novelli? I wondered) was evidently the name of the young tour guide, who had returned to the cellar. With amazing self-possession, Francesca told the story. I was starting to shiver in the cool cellar.

"Do you know who the guy is?" Baca asked.

She shook her head.

"Could he have been a tourist?" Baca continued.

"I don't think so," Francesca replied. "This was the first tour of the day."

"What about from yesterday? The guy's pretty cold—he's been here a while."

"I don't know. The last tour yesterday was at four o'clock. People usually come here in couples, or groups, and no one complained that anyone was missing. And if he was here since yesterday afternoon—I don't know if anyone came in here last night or not."

"Somebody did." Baca grinned wryly. He turned to Tom and me. "You two have anything to add?"

Neither of us did. Baca took Tom's address and phone number and told us we could leave. I thought about giving him mine as well, but I didn't want to emphasize that we weren't together.

I was glad to be back in the sunshine. I was still shivering.

"Can we sit for a minute?" I asked.

18

"Sure."

We walked over to the picnic tables on the lawn next to the winery. I chose one directly in the sun. Tom sat across from me.

"What now?" he asked.

"No picnic. I'm sorry, but I've kind of lost my appetite," I told him. "What do you think happened?"

He shrugged. "Guy probably had a heart attack."

"Come on. He was too young for that. And the vomit?"

"Sometimes young guys have heart attacks. I'm not a cop anymore. I don't care what happened."

"But somebody died. And we were there when the body was found. How can you not care? How can you just walk away from that?"

Tom shrugged again. "Baca seemed pretty competent."

We sat in silence. I didn't meet his gaze.

"Look," he finally added, "I know you're a writer, and you're curious. But don't even think about messing with this."

"What do you mean?"

"I mean you don't know what you're doing. And a one-day self-defense workshop doesn't mean shit when you're up against a murderer."

"You're saying that I'll be in trouble without you to save me, is that it?"

I felt mean and ungrateful even as I said it.

"No. I'm saying that maybe you see murder as a game, as a puzzle to be solved, the way you see the rest of life, and it isn't."

I thought about that. He was wrong. Someone had been murdered and I had been hurt—that was how this relationship had started. He had saved me, and he had wanted to heal my pain. I had really wanted to fall in love with him. But I hadn't seen any of it as a game.

"I think I want to go home," I said quietly.

"Home?"

"Home."

When we reached Tom's house, he unstrapped the ice

chest from the back of the Harley and put it on the passenger seat of my car. I wanted to tell him to take the food, but he was too far away for that. I went into the house and quickly threw my clothes into the two overnight bags. I wished I hadn't brought so much, hadn't intended to stay for a few days.

Tom was sitting on the front steps staring out. I stopped at the door. I felt a surge of anger at him, irrationally, because I was the one who was leaving, I was the one who wasn't in love. I strode past him and heaved my bags into the car.

"I'll call you," I said.

"What's this going to do to your story on the wine industry?"

"Probably nothing—I'll find out tomorrow when I talk with John Novelli."

"You're driving home now and coming back tomorrow?"

"Yes. That's when the appointment is."

"You're going to ask him about the body, not just the winery, aren't you?"

I stopped, but didn't say anything. I had been thinking about it, and I hated him knowing that.

"You asshole," he said.

"Goodbye. See you."

I slammed the door of the Alfa and started the car.

"See you," he said, with an edge.

He was still looking at me, and my stomach was knotted thinking about what I might say to him, all of it unfair. The tires screeched as I pulled out of the drive.

I took the turn from the road onto Highway 246 a little too fast and stomped harder on the accelerator, wanting to feel the power of the car. Just before I reached Lake Cachuma, I slowed to fifty-five. I had gotten a speeding ticket the month before and didn't want another one. Besides, I was calming down, losing the need to drive on the edge of recklessly.

As I rounded the curve where the ocean first became visible, clear blue, painfully bright from the sun, beyond a dark green valley between two brown, scrub-covered hills, I

20

slowed further. The view was whatever one called the opposite of breathtaking—I wanted to breathe more deeply, wanted to clear my head and my lungs and my heart.

By the time I got to Santa Barbara, I was feeling relaxed and hungry. I took the turnoff to the state beaches. Even though it was a weekday, the beach had a heavy August crowd. I found a parking space, moved my bags to the trunk of the car, and pulled out the old Indian blanket I kept there. I tucked the blanket under my arm, grabbed my handbag and the ice chest, and wandered toward the shore, toward that painfully bright water, until I saw a spot I liked, clean sand and not too close to anyone else.

I had finished as much as I wanted of the creamy shrimp and cucumber soup and was about to start on the chicken in tarragon sauce, the marinated broccoli with red onions, and the rice salad, wishing I had thought to pick up a bottle of wine, when Michelangelo's David (wearing trunks) materialized next to me, blond and bronzed and maybe twenty years old.

"Looks like you have enough for two," he said, with a smile that sent the blood rushing to my face.

"I probably have enough for four normal appetites, or for thee and me," I said dryly, remembering from my recent days in graduate school the way well-built young men could eat. "I don't suppose you brought anything to drink."

The smile remained. "Want a beer?"

"Sure," I said, smiling back.

He returned almost immediately with two Heinekens. It pays to come to a high-class beach.

I gave Russ—for that was his name—the rest of the soup and watched him pile chicken and broccoli and rice on his plate. I was right. There was just enough for the two of us. I handed him the French bread and the Brie and the wine-soaked peaches and raspberries.

"Thanks," he said, still smiling. "This is great. Do you come here often? I don't think I've seen you before."

I realized that the question was only to keep me talking

while he ate. I briefly explained my presence and my occupation, punctuated by a couple of "no kiddings" from Russ.

When he had finished, he stretched out on his side, propped up on one well-formed elbow, showing off his long, bronzed torso. "Want another beer?" he asked.

"No thanks," I replied. "I want to digest the food and then head on back to L.A."

"Can I talk you into sticking around for the afternoon? Maybe we could do something later, go to a movie."

"I don't think so," I said, pleased by the attention but not wanting to pursue it.

"That's okay," he said, the smile unwavering. "Sooner or later I would probably have called you Mom."

He hopped up and trotted away.

I felt the skin on my face drying, the lines around my eyes deepening, my breasts sagging, even as I watched him go. So much for the beautiful people. I packed the empty cartons in the ice chest, folded the old Indian blanket, and returned to the car.

Amazingly, the sun was still shining as I drove down the coast toward Los Angeles. After a few miles I even found the remark funny.

By the time I turned off the Hollywood Freeway onto Alvarado, and followed the circuitous streets to my house, I had had enough of the sun and the afternoon. And enough of the drive. I probably should have stayed in a motel. I was not looking forward to driving back the next day.

I retrieved my bags from the trunk, noted as I took the path around the large front house toward my smaller one in back that Norman had picked up my *Times* and my mail, stepped carefully up to the front door to avoid the peahen shit, and carefully unlocked the front door, disconnecting the alarm.

"Pretty bird," I called, and Salome ruffled her feathers in acknowledgment. Common slander would have it that peahens are plain. Peahens only seem plain if there is a male of their species around. Otherwise, their iridescent necks, spiky crests, and starkly painted black and white faces make them the fairest of them all. And Salome, who didn't have to forage for her supper, was a particularly beautiful example.

I dropped my bags on the despised red carpet in my living room—if I had known how many years I would live in that house, I would have torn up the carpet and refinished the floors when I moved in—headed for the kitchen to take care of the remains in the ice chest. A bath and a nap, that's what I needed.

The fan in the bedroom had not made a dent in the ovenlike atmosphere of the little blue stucco house when I finally lay down on the bed. I woke up groggy and uncomfortable and decided that the only way to handle the rest of the day was with a book in the backyard and a salad for dinner.

I had checked two books on California wines out of the public library some days earlier, and I took them with me to the large cushioned redwood chair under the grapefruit tree. I also took a glass of California Chardonnay—it was beginning to beat French wines in the $5–$6-per-bottle category in which I normally drank.

The cats were all in their places. Blaze, a long-haired half Siamese with white boots, was almost hidden in the ivy. Chandra, a long-haired sable cat, was under her chair. Chandra's boy, Bubba, who looked just like his mother, was in the trench I had dug to keep the grapefruit tree watered. Marcia, an unattractively mottled blue-cream calico, was never around during the day.

I couldn't concentrate on the books. First, the early evening was too hot to read anything but mysteries. Second, I was sweating and my clothes were sticking to my skin, and third, I was wondering about the body of the young man in the Novelli wine cellar. Would Baca want anything more from me? How could I find out more—if I wanted to? And, most important, would John Novelli still see me?

When I made the appointment with John Novelli for 10:30 A.M., I had done so with the idea that I would be sleeping at Tom's house, that I could have a leisurely—read "slow"—morning, the kind that made me glad I didn't work for anyone but myself. Now, to get there on time from Los Angeles, I would have to get up at six-thirty and keep moving, with no time for a second cup of coffee and the morning paper.

I slept fitfully that night, too warm under the sheet, hating to sleep with the fan on, the drone penetrating my dreams, becoming an electrical monster that chased me through the night. I turned it off about five o'clock, and fell promptly into a deep sleep that was politely interrupted by a Mozart sonata on the clock radio. I lay there listening, not wanting to move, knowing I was risking being late, and feeling too drained from the heat to care.

I was forced to get up because of an urgent pressure in my bladder. My muscles were less stiff, but I was certain middle age was upon me. Maybe even old age. On good days, of course, thirty-six is young.

As I brushed my teeth, I examined my face in the bathroom mirror. The shadows under my eyes were almost indigo—I knew they had passed the point of no return. They would never again go away after a good night's sleep. My skin would never again be clear and unlined. Five years of makeup and hot lights as a television newscaster had damaged it, and I probably hadn't helped it with sun worship. But I had a tan seldom seen outside of Palm Springs or Malibu, and that made up for a lot.

My eyes were an unusual light brown, my long, crinkly-permed hair dark brown with reddish blond highlights, although some of the highlights were now gray. During my three-year incarnation as a blonde (I had wanted to find out if it was true blondes had more fun, and I had thought blond hair might look better under the television lights), my friends had been surprised to discover how light my eyes were. My hair was so dark that people somehow thought of me with dark eyes as well.

I wasn't beautiful. But I was too strong-featured to be dismissed as merely pretty. Because of that, I was more attractive now than I had been when I was younger, when "cheerleader" was the look that everyone wanted. And I had

24

the kind of character in my face that caused heads to turn when I made an entrance.

Having decided that I could live with myself a little longer, I left the bathroom. I picked up the phone to check in with Fred Crossley, my editor at *Explore!*, to let him know the murder might delay the article. In New York, it was already a reasonable hour.

"You were right there? On the spot?" he wheezed.

"Even a little too close."

"That will certainly lend color to the article."

"Fred, I can't imagine you running a story about murder in the sleepy little village of Santa Clarissa. Repressed passions, wine flowing like blood, all of that."

"Not exactly our style, of course. Although if the corpse is anyone important, or if there's anything unusual about the murder, you might think about a book. Truman Capote, Shana Alexander, *Peyton Place,* and all that."

"Thanks for the idea. But first I owe you an article."

I hung up the phone, set aside fantasies, and returned to the task at hand—deciding what to wear, always a problem for me. Sometimes I change clothes two or three times before I like the way I look. I should have decided on clothes the night before. I wondered what would last through both the drive and the interviews—after the one I had formally set up with Novelli, I had planned some informal ones, just dropping in on some of the other wineries. Most of the owners were around during the hours the wineries were open to the public, I had discovered through a few phone calls. Novelli was an exception, which was why I had made the appointment.

I finally chose white cotton pants and vest and a pink cotton blouse. I added a hot pink belt and beads and sandals. I tossed makeup into an overnight bag and stuck a fuchsia jumpsuit (I was wearing a lot of pinks that summer) into a plastic garment bag, just in case I was too tired to drive home. I left a big bowl of Science Diet dry food for the cats, and a big bowl of fresh water, even though I knew I could call Norman from Santa Clarissa.

I gave Salome fresh water and tossed a handful of cat food into the dish of bird seed, calling "Pretty bird!" Salome came swiftly around the corner of the house, head and long neck first as always. She shook her feathers and squawked a bit as she climbed the stairs to the porch, surprised that breakfast was so early. I had discovered how much Salome liked cat food one day when I had offered food to a gorgeous white tomcat who had wandered into the yard looking beaten and forlorn. Salome chased him away from the food, and that was enough for him. Not wanting to stay in a yard ruled by a very large bird, he had decided to wander elsewhere.

I paused at the corner of the front house to look at the city in the morning light. When it was this comfortable at seven-thirty, one could count on a hot, smoggy day. But now it was still clear. Directly in front of me, the street sloped down to Sunset Boulevard. Not the glamorous part of Sunset, but the ethnic part, where Sunset curved downtown, where grocery stores had strange yellow squashes in the produce section, and most of the signs were in Spanish. My favorite window (I had never ventured inside the shop) belonged to an Iglesia Botanica. Painted plaster Madonnas sat serenely beside winged totems and strange masks. Once I had even seen a statue of Christ bearing Himself on a crutch—grotesque, really, a grade school joke realized, complete with bright red blood dripping from a crown of thorns.

On the other side of Sunset, the street again sloped up a hill covered with more small houses, all with the kind of individuality that disappeared in ones built after World War II. To the west were the high-rises of Hollywood and the more fashionable Hollywood Hills. The morning was so clear that I could see the mountains that defined the Los Angeles basin. The Griffith Park observatory gleamed.

The palm trees dotting the panoramic view seemed like comic relief. They were too tall for the small houses and too short for the skyscrapers. If I had been an angelic architect, I wouldn't have designed palm trees. I understood why people made fun of palm trees.

26

I turned back from the view to see Norman sitting on the steps, with a cigarette in his hand and a cup of coffee beside him, reading my newspaper. Helena wouldn't let him smoke in the house.

"Oh. I didn't hear you," Norman said, jumping to his feet. "I thought you were in Santa Clarissa."

"I was, and I will be again. But I'm pretty much going to be commuting, I think."

"Oh."

Norman didn't ask about Tom, and I didn't feel like volunteering. He started to refold the newspaper. I knew he often read my paper before I was up in the morning, and I marveled at the way he refolded it and put the string back around it so that it looked untouched.

"It's okay," I said. "I'll read it when I get back."

"No, I have to get going anyway. I have to check out an estate sale in Long Beach."

Norman was an antiques dealer. He had had a shop on Sunset for several years, but as the neighborhood changed, his business had suffered. He couldn't compete with Iglesia Botanica. He now spent his time at estate sales and swap meets.

"Well, have a good day in Long Beach. I hope it's cooler there."

He shrugged. "Not much. I envy you going to Santa Clarissa."

"Right. Thanks." I took the offered paper.

I was on the freeway and headed north by eight. The valleys were already so warm that I was shocked when I hit the coast—and the ocean fog—about nine-thirty, and the temperature dropped ten degrees. I hadn't been cool in so long that I was starting to forget what it felt like. Except in the wine cellar. I had been cool in the wine cellar.

The doll's head stared at me from the same green light in Santa Barbara. No one had retrieved it. I thought of the Cheshire Cat. But the doll wasn't smiling. I felt a chill and drove on as the light turned.

3

I pulled into the parking lot of the Novelli Winery about quarter to eleven. I was surprised to find it empty. And the dark heavy doors were locked. Belatedly, I noticed a hand-lettered sign that said "Closed Today—Please Come Back Tomorrow" taped over the tour schedule. I looked around, wondering what to do. I had been vaguely aware the day before that there was a house some distance beyond the winery. Doubtless Novelli expected me to come to the house—if he even remembered he had scheduled the inter-view. The house had a separate drive, but I decided that my pink sandals wouldn't be destroyed by a short walk through the grass.

The grass, of course, was damp—I should have guessed that it would be; it was the only way to keep it so green in the heat. Short of painting it. I was now less certain that my sandals wouldn't be ruined, but kept going.

The house was as white as the winery, but it didn't have

that movie-set Spanish look. It was designed to be wide open—like houses in Acapulco, where people lived outside most of the year and only locked the bedrooms and the kitchen. A car with the insignia of the Santa Clarissa County Sheriff was parked in front of the house. Three people were standing next to the car: Francesca, Baca, and another man.

I concentrated on the unknown man as I approached. The sun shone so brightly on his white hair that it was as if he gave light, rather than reflected it. He was in his fifties, about my own height, but heavier—sturdy was the word that came to mind—dressed in well-tailored white slacks and a pale blue shirt, open necked, the sleeves rolled casually. His weathered face was flushed beneath an olive tan. He was angry.

I was finally close enough to hear what he was saying—just in time to hear "Goodbye, Will," as he turned and strode into the house.

"Please, Papa—" Francesca shrugged and smiled at Baca. "I'm sorry, Will. You should have sent somebody else to talk to him."

"I'm here professionally, not personally. You'd think he could keep the two separate."

"Well, he can't."

They were suddenly aware of me. I was embarrassed at being caught so obviously eavesdropping. I quickly explained that I had an appointment to see John Novelli.

"Why?" Baca asked, appraising me.

"I'm doing an article," I fumbled. "I'm a writer." I turned to Francesca. "Morgan Reeves. That was why I came to the winery yesterday—research."

Francesca looked at me with clear brown eyes. "He's probably forgotten. I'm not sure he'll want to see you. But I'll ask. Come with me."

She held out her hand to Will Baca. I was impressed once more with her self-possession, when she looked so young.

"I guess we'll see you soon," Francesca said lightly.

Baca took her hand, held it. "I'm sorry, Francesca."

"I know. Goodbye."

Francesca started walking toward the house, not looking back. I hesitated and then followed. Baca didn't stop me.

I paused inside the open front door, not certain what to do next. There was an expanse of living room in front of me, all windows and stone and fireplace, with almost no furniture. Francesca returned.

"Come with me. He'll see you for a moment."

I followed Francesca into a room lined on three walls with floor-to-ceiling bookcases. The fourth wall was a window, looking out on the mountains. The white-haired man was standing behind a large teak desk, staring out the window. Silhouetted, his profile was sharp, hawklike.

"I'm terribly sorry," he said as he turned toward me. "A very unfortunate thing has happened, and I should have canceled the appointment, but I'm afraid I forgot all about it. Please forgive me. Would you mind if we rescheduled it for another time? You didn't drive all the way up from Los Angeles just to see me, did you? I hope not."

His voice was rich and deep and cultured, and I wanted to hear more. And then he looked up, and I saw his eyes. I had expected him to have dark eyes, like his daughter. I was startled to see that his eyes were bright blue, as sharply bright as yesterday's ocean in the sun. My heart lurched a little. He reminded me of someone I used to know. Know well, in fact. But where my onetime lover's eyes had been gentle, the lines of his face soft, this man's eyes were hard, the lines deep. And this man's mouth was full and hard and sensual. Cruel? I wasn't sure. And I wasn't likely to find out. I set aside the memories, cleared my head.

"Of course we can reschedule," I told him, still a little flustered, not just because of the resemblance, but because he was strikingly handsome in his own right. As I looked, he began to remind me less of my ex-love and more of an Italian actor whose name I couldn't remember. I relaxed a bit. "I was here yesterday. I was on the tour—when the body was discovered."

"Then you know what happened," he said, gesturing oddly,

vaguely with his hands. "I don't know what more I can say."

"Yes. I'm sorry. It must be terribly upsetting for you—someone dead in your wine cellar. I wonder—since I happened to be there—" I stopped, certain that I seemed morbidly curious. "I'm sorry. Why don't we just schedule the interview for another time?"

He raised his eyebrows. "That must have been terribly upsetting for *you*, discovering a body."

"Yes. Yes, it was."

He nodded. Then he picked up a book-size calendar from the desk, leafed through a few pages, sighed, and shook his head.

"It doesn't look good. We're going to have to talk now. Why don't we take a walk?"

"Okay," I said, thinking briefly but wistfully of my pink sandals and the damp grass. I noted that he was wearing white canvas loafers.

But we didn't go out the front door. He steered me with a firm hand on my elbow out a back door of the house, toward a trail that led gently up the hillside.

"Tell me again who you are and why you wanted to talk to me," John said as we reached the path.

I explained about *Explore!*, that the magazine popularized science, including the social sciences, that I was a contributing editor, and that they wanted an article about the Santa Clarissa wineries.

"This is the first of several visits," I told him. "I'll be back with a photographer, of course. It's so beautiful here."

He smiled, a full, white-toothed smile. I was conscious of his mouth, of his full lower lip. "You should be here in October, for the concert and general celebration at the end of the harvest."

I smiled back. "I expected to finish the article before October, but maybe I ought to delay it to include the celebration. That sounds like a good idea."

"What do you need to know today?"

I needed to know who the dead man was and why John

31

Novelli had blue eyes and if he had any idea who the killer was and what had happened between John and Will Baca, but I wasn't sure how to ask some of those questions and couldn't possibly ask the others.

"I'd like to know as much as you'll tell me about yourself and about the winery."

We rounded a curve and the sun fell on his white hair. I stopped to look at him. He misunderstood.

"A little way ahead there's a clearing with a bench. If you don't want to walk and talk at the same time, we can sit there."

"No," I said, embarrassed. "It's all right."

But he led me to the bench in silence. The clearing also held a barbecue pit and some picnic tables. We were once again in the shade—it was too hot to sit in the sun, for which I was grateful. I didn't want to talk with him while the sun shone on his hair.

"Well, to start with, I was born March eighth, 1935, at St. Mary's Hospital in Philadelphia. I weighed six pounds, four ounces, and my mother says it was a difficult birth. Shall I go on from there? I have to warn you, I'm quite willing to tell you everything about myself. But I'm afraid that if I do, I can't possibly get to the time I bought the winery before Sunday—talking steadily." His delivery was so deadpan that I had to search his eyes to find his amusement. The eyes weren't as hard as I had first thought.

"Okay," I said. "Cut to the chase."

"What?"

"It's a movie term. I'm saying let's go straight to the exciting part of the story."

"You were in the movies? You're an actress, aren't you." He looked at me intently.

"Not since college, but I was on television—a newscaster—and it's really all the same industry. But now I'm a writer. And I'm not here to talk about me."

"No, of course not. We'll do that later. Are you free for dinner? We could talk about you then."

32

My heart flipflopped. I had a brief flash of what it would be like, allowing myself to be seduced by this man. The thrill of the dance. I smiled, wanting to shake my hair loose and fall into his arms. I wanted to touch his hard, generous mouth. All over my body, I wanted to touch it.

"Yes, I'm free for dinner," was all I said.

"Good. I bought this land ten years ago."

"What?"

"This is the exciting part of the story." He let his amusement show, finally, and I started to chuckle. "Isn't this what you want to hear?"

"Absolutely," I said, laughing. "This is exactly what I want to hear."

"My fantasy for twenty years—my entire adult life, from the moment I discovered wine—had been to own a vineyard and a small winery. Since I believe in living out my fantasies, I bought the land as soon as I reached a point where I could divide my energies between my business in Los Angeles and the life I wanted to build here. I planted the vines and built the house, moved my wife, my daughters, and my father here, and began several years of commuting, driving up here Thursday night and leaving again on Monday morning. Only the vines and the house turned out as I planned them."

"What does that mean?"

"My wife discovered that she missed the city—and she didn't miss me. Solitude held no pleasures for her, and she had no desire to be the queen of the Santa Clarissa vintners. I gave her the house in Los Angeles as part of the settlement, and I think both of us are happier, really. My daughters—actually, I misspoke a moment ago. The vines, the house, and Francesca turned out as I planned. Francesca turned out better, in fact. She has quite a head for marketing and promotion. She designed the gift shop, and she stocks it and runs it. In fact, she's the general manager of the whole operation."

"She looks so young. How old is she?"

"She's twenty-six. Her maturity is remarkable, however.

Not that my other daughter, Eva, isn't remarkable in her own way."

"Was she the other young woman in the gift shop?"

"No. That was Diane, Francesca's friend. She works for us part-time. Eva doesn't live with us. And my father is old now, which shouldn't be a disappointment, but it reminds me of my own mortality."

"Does that mean you don't want to say any more about Eva?"

"That's right. At least not now. In fact, I can't say anything more now. I have to get back. Can you meet me at the house at seven-thirty? Is that convenient for you?"

"Of course." As we rose and started back down the trail, I added impulsively, "You said that you believed in living out your fantasies. What's your fantasy now?"

John stopped and turned to me. "Why, you, of course. A man is killed in my wine cellar and the body is discovered by a beautiful woman who wants to ask me questions. The game, as they say, is afoot."

I blushed.

"But the questions I want to ask you are about winemaking. Ones like why you decided to plant Pinot Noir grapes."

He nodded. "That one I can answer easily. I was smart enough—and lucky enough—to be one of the first to realize that this valley has the same climate and much the same soil as the Bordeaux region of France. California white wines were starting to gain international recognition, and there was no reason why our red wines couldn't as well. I could have planted Cabernet grapes, of course, but others were doing that. Besides, no Bordeaux wine has the power of a good Burgundy. I found a young winemaker who wanted to experiment, and we were on our way."

"I'll want to talk with him, too."

"Phil Grademon. You'll find him at his own winery."

"Has he left you?"

"No—it's not unusual for a winemaker to work for himself as well as a larger winery. Not that ours is much larger."

"You said he wanted to experiment—how?"

"That, my dear, requires a very long answer. The intricacies of winemaking must wait for another time."

He took my hand and placed it inside his arm, so that we could walk together. We did so in silence, touching. Breathing deeply, I could almost smell his body. I wanted to nuzzle his ear. Instead, I asked another question.

"Is the murder going to cause problems for the winery?"

"I hope not—one can't tell, of course. But if Will does his job—if this is taken care of quickly—there shouldn't be anything that we can't handle with some good public relations. After all, the murder doesn't really have anything to do with the winery, except that the body was found here. There's no scandal behind this. The only connection is that Eva knew the murdered man—Rick Clarence his name was—years ago, at U.C. Davis, but she hadn't been in touch with him."

I froze. "A body was found in your wine cellar, and your daughter knew the man. How can you be certain the murder doesn't have anything to do with the winery?"

He turned, flared. Blue eyes riveted mine.

"Because my family lives here, and this small piece of land that is now my home is the most important thing in my life. If something were wrong, I would know."

"I'm sure you're right," I said, stumbling over the words. "And it isn't as if there were something wrong with the wine."

"What?" He seemed stunned.

"I just meant—I think there was some kind of scandal a few years ago, pesticides in Italian wine, and nobody would drink Italian wine because of it."

"Never! No one in this valley, in this state, would use pesticides on grapes!"

He was momentarily furious, and I was wildly trying to come up with a way to get out of the mess I had just stepped in, but his face softened almost immediately. He patted my hand and we resumed walking.

When we got back to the house, he stopped at the door and

said, "I would invite you in, but I must get some work done today. I'll see you here at seven-thirty."

"I understand," I said, not wanting to move from the spot. "Um, actually, I have work to do, too. There are some other wineries I plan on hitting today."

"Good. Until later, then." He took the hand that was still tucked into his arm, kissed the fingers lightly, and dropped it.

I watched him walk into the house and shut the door. I closed my eyes and tried to erase his image.

The next step was to get a room. I was glad I had brought a change of clothes—but I wished it was something other than the jumpsuit.

I started around the house, back toward the winery parking lot and my car, and discovered a shaded patio. An elderly man in a wheelchair was sitting beside a small glass-topped table with a glass of water, some medicine bottles, and a large bell on it. The man had John Novelli's white hair, but thinner—I could see liver spots on his scalp—and blue eyes, and the same hawk nose, but his skin was untanned, and he had a full white mustache. His arms and face were thin, but his stomach was distended, as if all of his flesh had settled around a middle that his white shirt could barely cover. He wore dark slacks and open sandals, and his socks didn't match—one was light blue and soft, the other an ordinary navy blue. As I stood there, the pale blue eyes slowly turned toward me.

"Hello," I said. "Mr. Novelli?"

He nodded slowly. "Hi," he whispered.

"Hi. I'm Morgan Reeves. I came here to interview your son for an article on winemaking."

He nodded again and gestured toward the chair on the other side of the table. I climbed the few stairs to the patio and sat in the cushioned, wrought-iron chair.

"Do you want something to drink?" he whispered. He had to form his words carefully. I guessed he had suffered a stroke, or a series of strokes. He focused his wide blue eyes—not as deep or as dark as John's—with the same care that he formed his words.

36

"Yes, thank you," I said, suddenly aware of my thirst in the warmth of the morning. "If it's not too much trouble," I added.

He shook his head and picked up the bell. It clanged loudly, like an old school bell. A short, stout, full-breasted woman in a white uniform and a professional smile appeared almost immediately.

"What do you need, Tony?" she asked cheerfully. She raised her eyebrows slightly as she noticed me.

"Bring her a glass of the 1985 Pinot Noir Reserve," Tony whispered.

The woman's eyebrows rose a little higher.

"Oh, no, please, it's too early," I spluttered. "A glass of water will be fine."

"Are you sure?"

"Really—I'd love to try the Pinot Noir another time—I promise."

He nodded. "Okay." He turned to the white-uniformed woman. "Bring her a glass of Perrier, with ice and a twist." The woman retreated through the French doors at the back of the patio. Tony turned back to me and smiled, a full, child's smile. "I keep up, you know."

"I'm sure you do," I said, smiling in return.

"That's Lucy. She takes care of me. If you need anything while you're here, let her know."

"I will," I replied, lowering my voice to match his.

"Are you married?"

"No."

"And you met my son?"

"Yes."

He nodded again. "Good. He's not married either." And he smiled again, that wonderful smile, strange, full and empty at the same time.

"I *just* met your son, and I don't really think I'm going to marry him," I said, as Lucy appeared with my Perrier.

Tony motioned me to be quiet.

"Here you are," Lucy said. "Is there anything else you need?"

"Thank you, that's fine," I said.

Lucy seemed surprised to be thanked. Tony gestured with his good hand in the same vague way that his son had with both hands, and Lucy left.

"I don't want Lucy to know everything. She tells Eva. Have you met Eva?"

"Not yet. I've met Francesca."

He nodded. "Good. If Francesca approves of you, that's good. You'll have to meet Eva, though."

I reached out and placed my hand on top of the dried one resting on the arm of the wheelchair.

"Tony, I don't think anybody has to approve of me. I mean, nobody ever has. Why should they start now?"

"I approve of you." He was serious.

"I appreciate that, I really do. But you don't know me. And I don't want you to get any ideas about your son and me. I'm here on business."

He laughed. "Good. Tell that to Eva."

"Is she here?"

Tony shook his head. "No. She's not here very often. Sometimes she brings Johnny."

"Johnny?"

"My great-grandson."

"Eva's married?"

Tony shook his head again. "Divorced. I think they're divorced, anyway. Lucy can tell you." He started to reach for the bell.

"No, that's okay." I stopped him. "Who was Eva married to?"

"Will. Have you met Will?"

"Will Baca?"

Tony nodded.

"Yes," I said. "I've met Will."

"Good man. Eva shouldn't have left him."

"Why did she?"

He shrugged his shoulders. "I don't know. But it wasn't right. She shouldn't have left him."

"If I wanted to meet Eva, where would I find her?"

"Ranch. Near Buellton. Not too far."

"Thanks." I finished my Perrier. "And thanks for the Perrier. I needed that."

Tony laughed. "Will you come back and see me?"

"Of course I will."

"Because of John?"

"No. Because of you."

I kissed him on his forehead. He smelled dusty.

He laughed some more. "Oh, I wish I were forty years younger."

"If you were, you'd be too young for me." I winked at him. "I'll see you later. I still want that glass of 1985 Pinot Noir Reserve."

"You got it," he said.

We waved at each other as I walked around the corner of the house. The lawn was already dry in the heat, and I cut across it to the winery parking lot without worrying about my sandals.

I drove to the small gas station—three pumps, one of each—half a mile from the winery that signaled the start of the Santa Clarissa business district. The station was attached to a grocery store about the size of a converted outhouse. On the corner were a newspaper rack and a telephone booth, the old-fashioned kind that Superman changed in.

I picked up a Santa Clarissa Valley *Gazette*, handed the station attendant a quarter, and asked him where I might have lunch, although I didn't have much faith in his recommendation.

My distrust wasn't justified. He directed me to a clean, bright, family-owned coffee shop a few blocks away. My egg salad sandwich was served on thick dark bread with a small bowl of fresh fruit. While I waited for the young, fresh-faced, ponytailed waitress to serve me, I looked through the paper for the story about the body at the winery.

There wasn't much. Rick Clarence had died from pesticide poisoning, late Monday night or early Tuesday morning. The sheriff was investigating. No wonder John was so upset when I made that remark about pesticides in the wine. But pesticides had to be fairly common in this area. They were probably used on everything but grapes and horses.

I skimmed the rest of the paper as I finished my sandwich and iced tea. The only local excitement was a horse show scheduled for the coming weekend.

The sheriff's office was only a block away, so I walked.

Will was seated at his desk. He stood up as I entered.

I explained my presence. "I had thought I'd be staying up here, but since I'm not, I thought you might need to know how to get in touch with me, or want a formal statement."

"Thanks," he said. "But Molinez will testify at the coroner's inquest. So unless you saw something you haven't told us about, I don't think we'll need you."

Molinez. He meant Tom. I had almost forgotten about Tom.

"I don't think I saw anything except the body. The paper says you've identified him."

"Yeah—in fact I knew him, a long time ago."

"At Davis?"

The question, really a blurt, startled him and embarrassed me.

"Well, yes. I didn't really know him well, but I remembered his face." He paused, then grinned. "Novelli. He told you his daughter knew Rick Clarence at Davis. That's where you came up with the university. Who connected Eva with me?"

"Tony." Now I was truly embarrassed.

"Tony's a great old guy—I like him a lot, always have. I try to drop by and talk with him sometimes, but not as much as I'd like."

"You seem pretty relaxed about this."

Will laughed. "It's a front. Actually, it's kind of a tight spot."

He walked over and stared out the window for a moment, then continued. "A body is found in my former father-in-law's wine cellar, poisoned by parathion, a common pesticide. My ex-wife knew the guy, and so did at least a couple of other people in the valley. I don't know what the guy was doing here, who he came to see, I don't know if he was still at Davis, still a scientist, and I have no idea what he was working on before he bought the farm." Will shook his head. "You wanna be me?"

I shook my head in return. "Sounds as if you have a lot of work to do."

Will grinned. "Yeah, sounds that way. But don't worry, lady. We'll get 'im. We'll get the guy who done it."

Will should have been an actor. He liked playing his part so much.

"Or her?" I asked sweetly.

"What?"

"You're sure it's a man?"

Will glowered, losing a shred of his actor's cockiness.

"I've lived here a long time. I know the people up here well. I don't think the perp is a woman."

I felt dismissed, and I didn't have any reason to stay. I couldn't help wondering if Will's feelings for his ex-wife, whatever they were, would interfere in his investigation. Or his feelings for anyone else involved. I hoped not.

My next stop was the Cahill Winery. Although the output was about the same as the Novelli Winery, the Cahills didn't do anywhere near the same kind of promotion. No gift shop, no tours. The tasting room was a barn, with cases of wine stacked on three sides of a rectangular table with a few open bottles and a case of glasses.

On my way in, I stopped to say hello to a long-haired ginger cat lying in the shade. A blackboard propped on one end of the table listed the wines available for tasting.

The only person in the room turned out to be Alida Cahill, a woman in her early forties, with short salt-and-pepper hair brushed back from her sharp features. She was a little shorter,

41

a little heavier than I, wearing a loose, dark silk shirt and matching pants, and too much makeup for the day and place. The makeup didn't help her to look younger. And it didn't disguise the puffiness around her eyes, dark eyes with a soft focus. I wondered if Alida had been sampling her own product.

"I don't do very much promotion because I don't need to," she said in answer to my question. "There are a couple of places in Los Angeles that take all the wine we make. I may have to do more someday, as we expand, but I've learned to be careful. Too much of the time the tourists drink what's free and don't buy anything."

"I'm sure that's a problem," I agreed. I told her I wanted whatever information she could give me about the winery and the community.

"I'm not sure there's much of a community. The winemakers keep to themselves," Alida said. "So do the horsebreeders. None of us socialize very much. And the winemakers don't socialize with the horsebreeders."

"How unsociable are you? Isn't there even any gossip about the murder at the Novelli Winery?" I asked.

Alida laughed. "There's enough gossip about the Novellis without a murder. John's a notorious womanizer—he's rumored to have been to bed with everyone in the valley. Not *moi*, by the way, although he tried. His wife left him over his affairs—and his daughters hate men. Or at least Eva does."

I winced at her reference to John, although I had to admit I wasn't surprised. "What about Francesca?" I prompted.

Alida looked at me curiously, slightly amused. "If she does anything but worship Papa, no one knows about it."

"What makes you say Eva hates men?"

I was thinking of Will, who had seemed so likable.

"What does all this have to do with your story on the wine industry?"

Before I could come up with an answer, a young man burst in, saying, "Hey, Mom, the Mercedes won't start. I need the Auto Club card."

He stopped short when he saw me, then grinned. "Not *your* Auto Club card. Got another picnic?"

"Not today, Russ," I said dryly.

"You've met?" Alida asked, now wary.

"Only at the beach," I replied, ignoring Alida's raised eyebrows. But it was time to leave.

"Thank you for your help. I may be back later—I may be back with a photographer, to get some pictures of the harvest, if that's all right."

"That would be fine," Alida said. "As you may have heard, harvest really is the most interesting thing that happens around here. The only interesting thing. Except for murder, of course."

"Of course."

I made my goodbyes. The long-haired ginger cat let me pet him on my way out.

I went on to the Grademon Winery, losing my way and driving about three miles on the wrong mountain road before I backtracked and asked for directions at the gas station. The Grademon tasting room looked much like the Cahill one. But the house near the Cahill Winery had been very much post–World War II ranch style. The house here was Victorian, in the process of being restored.

The young man behind the table had definitely been sampling his own product. He was very drunk and very gay, no doubt about either. Drinking must be an occupational hazard in Santa Clarissa. He was young, tall, tanned and darkly mustached, wearing only khaki shorts and an unbuttoned cotton shirt.

"What would you like?" he asked, smiling.

"I don't know—what's good?" I countered.

Again, I was the only tourist on a slow weekday.

"Everything is good. Everything I want I've got," he said without blinking, holding his hands out to display the wealth around him.

"You," I said, "are a very fortunate fellow."

"Yeah, I am," he responded with a drunken smile. "And I'm going to keep it, too."

I glanced at the blackboard. "White Zinfandel?"

He splashed a bit in the bottom of a wine glass and handed it to me. "Yuppie Kool-Aid."

"I know that. I was surprised you even made it."

I dumped it on the floor near the drain where a lot of other tastes had obviously been poured and placed the glass on the table.

"Do you recommend anything?"

He laughed, almost a titter. "Try our 1988 Sauvignon Blanc. You might like that one."

I found it a bit acidic, but otherwise okay. "How long have you been here?"

"Since a little before noon."

"Let me try again. How long has the Grademon Winery been here?"

"Phil's father staked him in 1985."

"Phil? Phil Grademon?"

"Phil Grademon, owner and vintner. But he was the vintner at the Novelli Winery for four years before that. Phil has always loved wine—his degree from Davis is in oenology."

Davis again. Phil Grademon was probably one of the others Baca mentioned who had known the murdered man.

"Do you and Phil live in the house?"

"Yeah. There's a lot to do around here. We aren't even close to finished with the house yet."

"Is Phil here? Could I talk to him?"

"Not today. Not today." He had hesitated, and his voice sounded a little more sober.

I was wondering if I could get any useful information from him when two couples, cousins to the polyester woman and the heavy man who had been at the Novelli Winery the day before, walked in, and the young man turned his charming, drunken smile on them.

"Hi," he said to them. "What would you like?"

He waved goodbye. I nodded and left.

Normally I wouldn't have been able to afford it, but since *Explore!* would be paying my expenses, I drove to Santa Clarissa's one hotel, the Mission Inn. It had apparently been designed by the same architect who had done the movie-set Spanish of the Novelli Winery. But in fact, the design was authentic enough that the lobby was cool, the way missions are cool. I liked the rough Mexican tile on the floors, the kind that chips and discolors and keeps looking better as it ages.

I liked the cool shower even more. My room was comfortably old-fashioned, with a four-poster bed and an oak dresser with a mirror. The heat had exhausted me, and I decided to take a nap, just a short one before dinner.

I set my travel alarm for seven and curled up on the bed.

4

I found the driveway leading from the winery to the house, and turned into it about quarter to eight. I had changed into my jumpsuit and cleaned my sandals as best I could, wishing I had brought another pair.

John was waiting at the door. He, too, had changed, but he was wearing essentially the same style shirt and pants plus a pale blue sport coat—the mountains were cool in the evening, no matter how hot the day had been.

"Good, you're here," he said. "I was going to ask you in for a glass of wine, but I made our reservation for eight-thirty, so perhaps we'd better leave. The restaurant's in Santa Barbara. I hope that's all right."

He had taken my hand and was looking intently at me as he spoke. I was close enough to him that if I breathed deeply, I could just catch the scent of his body beneath the light cologne. He smelled right—I wanted more.

"Of course it's all right."

"Good. I have a couple of books for you. One is background on California wines, the other is an introduction to winemaking. They may be too basic—I don't know how much work you've done already. Let me know what else you need. Or next time you're here just look through the shelves and take what you want."

"Thank you," I said as he handed them to me.

"Do you mind if we take your car?" he asked, steering me out and shutting the door.

"Not at all. I like to drive. But I have an Alfa, and the top's down. Do you mind sports cars?"

"No—in fact, I used to have an Alfa. But you'll be cold. Would you like to borrow a jacket?"

"Thank you, but I keep one in the trunk of the car."

He waited while I retrieved my old Ferrari jacket, a gift from a long-ago lover who had raced them. We got into the car, and I tucked my hair into a cap.

"I like that," he said. "I like the way you look."

"Thank you," I said again, wondering if I would spend the evening saying "thank you" to him.

We were high enough in the hills to catch the last of the sunset as we made the turn that revealed a sudden flash of ocean. The colors were pastels, pinks and lilacs, softer than the fiery reds of Los Angeles smogsets. The air was still warm, and I drove slowly, savoring the excitement of the moment.

When we reached Santa Barbara, he directed me to a quiet street off State Street and told me to park in front of an old brown Victorian house with a small sign that barely proclaimed it a restaurant. The mixture of the Spanish and the Victorian in this part of California always intrigued me. Inside, it was more formal than I would have expected. I felt woefully underdressed.

A maître d' in black tie greeted John by name and showed us to a small table in an alcove near a fireplace with a display that gave light but not heat. The room must once have been a large living room. I had glimpsed other rooms with tables, too, although I guessed that the house probably didn't seat many people, particularly compared to some Los Angeles restaurants.

"Do you want a drink?" John asked once we were seated.

I shook my head. "I'll be perfectly happy with wine."

"Good."

Without checking a wine list, he ordered a bottle from the maître d', who nodded and replied, "Very good, Mr. Novelli." He returned almost immediately with a bottle that he held for inspection. John put on a pair of Ben Franklin glasses, checked the label, and nodded. The maître d' opened and John tasted, a perfunctory taste. He nodded again. The maître d' poured two glasses about half full, with a flourish.

"This isn't from your winery," I said.

"No. This is from a northern California winery, and I hate admitting it, but it's better than any Chardonnay we've produced so far. We're still working on it."

I tasted it. It was without doubt the best white wine I had ever had.

A young waiter with a generic resemblance to Russ Cahill appeared bearing a blackboard with the menu written on it, propped on an easel. He explained the specials with delight.

"What would you like?" John asked softly.

"I want the lotte with the scallops and mussels and spinach and whatever the sauce was."

"Do you want an appetizer?"

I savored the thought. "I want the tuna sashimi and I want the asparagus vinaigrette, and I can't decide. Would you like to split them?"

"I'd love to," he said. "And I'll have the grilled swordfish." He paused until the waiter left and continued, "Now. Tell me how you spent your day."

"I stopped by to see Will Baca, went to the Cahill Winery, then the Grademon Winery."

He groaned. "Alida Cahill. I was probably thoroughly tarred."

"Not really. And you certainly weren't feathered. We didn't talk that much about you—although she felt it necessary to let me know that you have something of a reputation with women."

"I'm sure she did." John shook his head and took a sip of wine. "I must say that it's an exaggerated reputation. I don't think I've seduced half the women rumor would have you believe. I would have had to devote my life to seduction, given up work, everything. And while I love women—I admit that—I do have other interests. I also must admit to a brief and really rather minor fling with Alida right after my wife left, for which she's never forgiven me. And I'm sorry—I'd rather have had her for a friend."

"Alida said nothing happened between you. Why would she lie?"

"Why not, when you had just met her?"

I shrugged. "One of my strengths as an interviewer is that I seem to inspire self-disclosure in people. They don't often lie to me, and she didn't seem to be. But I suppose there could be some sort of denial going on, particularly if it ended badly."

"You've studied psychology, haven't you?"

"No, I haven't." I laughed, a little embarrassed. "Although I know I sound that way sometimes. I did graduate work in organizational behavior, which is kind of the psychological side of management."

"Why did you choose that?"

"God only knows. It seemed like a good idea at the time— in fact, it seemed like an ultimately rational idea at the time. I had decided I wanted to leave television, and graduate school was a way to drop out while I figured out what I wanted to do. Since organizations are where most people spend most of their lives, I had some kind of an idea that I could make a contribution studying what happened in the interface between person and institution. What actually happened is that I realized, rather painfully at the time, that I had to find a way to make a living outside of any institution— including the university."

"So you're a writer. You're still studying people and institutions."

"I write about them. But I don't pretend to study them."

"My daughter Eva would tell you that in general women must learn to make their livings on their own, outside male-dominated, hierarchical institutions. You're just one of the pioneers."

"What?"

"Eva is a therapist—a feminist therapist."

He smiled a bit sadly as he said it.

"That sounds all right. Why are you disappointed in her?"

"I'm not disappointed. Although there was a time when I hoped she would be my winemaker. And I'm sorry she has chosen to separate herself from all men, not just from Will and from me." He stopped, looked at me, then went on. "She was married to Will Baca."

"Yes, I know. I spoke briefly with your father, and he told me."

John leaned back in his chair and crossed his arms. "While you definitely inspire self-disclosure, I think you may be finding out too much too soon."

"Better than too little, too late," I said lamely.

The waiter arrived with the tuna sashimi, which was stacked with crisp won ton wrappers, sprinkled with sprouts and drizzled with a light mustard sauce, and the asparagus vinaigrette, which fanned out from a puff pastry horn.

"Which goes where?" he asked cheerfully.

"It doesn't matter," I said.

He gave me the tuna and John the asparagus. I cut the stack neatly in half, and chuckled as he carefully counted half the asparagus spears. I have stayed slender only through sheer willpower—deep inside me is a fat woman crying to get out.

"We don't have to talk about your family if you don't want to," I continued. "Let's talk about the wine industry."

"No, let's talk more about you. Why are you writing about the wine industry? What possible interest could you have in it?"

I sighed. "I'm being paid to write about it, and at least I have an interest in wine—I drink it. Some things I'm paid to write about I have no interest in whatsoever."

"Can't you make a living writing what you want to write?"

I was silent for a moment, taking another bite of the tender, raw tuna in its tangy dressing. "I don't know yet. I've started a book. And it's difficult, writing for someone else and writing for yourself, too. There are days when I think I'd rather hang wallpaper for a living than write things I don't want to write. It's as if I get smaller when I write for someone else, less creative, even less intelligent."

"Tell me about your book—the one you're writing for yourself."

"I don't think so. I don't trust you that much."

"Whom do you trust that much?"

"Nobody, right now."

"I hope you decide I'm all right—despite Alida. I would like to read your book."

He had eaten his share of the asparagus in large bites, showing square, white teeth, obviously enjoying it. I reached out to trade plates with him.

"I'll have to think about it. Besides, how can I trust somebody to read my book—why should I trust him at all—after a man was murdered in his wine cellar, by person or persons unknown?"

"I suppose Alida thinks I'm guilty of that, too."

"I don't know—I didn't ask her. Are you?"

"No, of course not." He seemed amused at the question.

"Why do you find that amusing?"

"I'm amused that you trust me enough to think I'll tell you the truth about whether I've committed a murder, but not enough to talk with me about your work."

"But those are different kinds of trust. And I told you, I expect people to tell the truth about themselves."

"True. You did say that. You must be very disappointed sometimes."

I looked at him, at the blue eyes and the black brows, the

square jaw, the deep lines that were lighter than his tan. The cruel mouth. I couldn't read his eyes, and I wondered if he were capable of murder.

"You're less upset about the murder than you were this morning."

"I'm not happy about it, certainly—it's not good for the tourist trade. Particularly since the agent was parathion. Any time pesticides are mentioned in the same context as wine, the publicity is bad. And I'm going to have to tolerate Will hanging around much more than I would like. He seems to think someone connected with the winery did it."

"I can guess why."

"Go ahead." He was amused again.

"First of all, the dead man was found in the wine cellar on the first tour of the day. He couldn't have been lying there dead since the last tour the day before, so he somehow got in—or was let in—at night. There was parathion and wine in his stomach, so he was drinking with the person who poisoned him—probably in the wine cellar, or somewhere near enough that he was dragged there before he died, since there was enough vomit around to indicate that he did in fact die in the wine cellar. Unfortunately for you—which also deflects suspicion from you personally, by the way—the parathion was probably in the wine. And the murdered man knew at least two people connected with the Novelli Winery—Phil Grademon and Eva Novelli."

"Yes. Will suspects that Phil did it somehow. That will be difficult to prove, since Phil was in Long Beach for a wine tasting all day. I think Will wouldn't want to suspect Eva. Besides, I don't believe Eva has a key to the winery any longer."

"But you're not sure."

"No."

"You could ask her."

"I could. But I suppose I don't want to suspect her either. She said she hadn't seen Rick Clarence since they were at Davis together. And I believe that."

"If he wasn't meeting Phil or Eva—what was the man doing in your wine cellar?"

"I think you're trusting me more and more. What makes you think I'll tell you the truth?"

The blue eyes were beguiling, if not exactly innocent, and I had to smile at him.

"I think you'll tell me the truth. Because if you don't, I'll probably find it out from someone else—or it will be in the paper, when the murder is solved—and then you will have betrayed my trust awfully early in the relationship."

"You're right. So I'll tell you the truth. I have no idea what Rick Clarence was doing in my wine cellar. I have no idea what he was doing in Santa Clarissa. I do know that he had some kind of clinical position at Davis, he wasn't on the faculty, and I know what he had been working on—it was a spectrometer that detected pesticides in fruit and vegetables. Considering the current emphasis on eating healthy, particularly in southern California, the device has quite a potential value for marketing with some of the larger agricultural concerns. He had kept in touch with Phil, and Phil mentioned it to me. Besides, it was written up in the L.A. *Times*."

"I must have missed it," I said wryly.

"No doubt."

"If nobody had seen the man in years, do you suppose something happened at Davis? Is this an old grudge?"

"I don't know that either. I don't think Eva knew Clarence well. And I haven't asked about Phil's relationship with him. Before you ask, I'm not curious."

He held up his hand to stop the question.

"Why not? You are about other things."

"Only things that directly concern me. Or people I want to get to know better. I have little intellectual curiosity, and, unlike you and Eva, I left the university life rather quickly."

"Do you want to tell me about it?"

"There isn't much to tell—I simply discovered that my talents were worth more on the open market."

"What's your most valuable talent?"

"A sense of value—I know what things are worth."

The eyes again. Caught.

The waiter broke the spell, as he arrived with the lotte and the swordfish and retrieved the other dishes.

I took a sip of that wonderful wine before I touched the lotte. The lotte melted in my mouth.

"This is great," I said. "You have to try it."

"I know—I've had it before. Would you like some of the swordfish?"

"No, this is all I want. I tried to catch Phil today, for my winemaking article, but he wasn't in. Will he be around tomorrow?"

"He'll probably be at the Grademon Winery tomorrow. I'll be curious to see how you do with him—I don't think he's likely to open up to you the way you expect people to."

"We'll see. I'll let you know if he starts volunteering information about old classmates."

"Not only do I not like to be gossiped about, I don't like to hear or repeat gossip. If he tells you anything material, pass it on to Baca."

"Why doesn't Will suspect you?"

"Perhaps he does. Perhaps he just didn't mention it to me."

"Is he a smart man? Do you think he'll solve this?"

"Yes. Why, have you decided you suspect me?" John shook his head, still faintly amused. "And I thought you were starting to trust me."

"I am—sort of. You had the opportunity, didn't you?"

"Yes. But I think you will find I had no motive."

"What makes you think I'm going to check?"

"How can you really trust me if you don't?"

He was so relaxed about it. And amused. How could he be guilty of murder and be so relaxed? I tried to read the blue eyes again.

"I'll have to think about it."

"Fine. While you're considering your trust, I have another question. Do you like theater?"

"Yes."

"I thought you might. I have to be in Los Angeles on Sunday for a wine tasting. I could drive down on Saturday and take you to the theater. What would you like to see?"

I noted that he hadn't asked if I were available. And that he had changed the subject. "Is that all you guys do? Go to wine tastings?" I countered.

"I know you think it's fun—outsiders always do. But it's a bore. I'm hoping you'll go with me to the tasting, too, to save it for me."

"I'll think about it. Are you judging?"

"No," he said, chuckling deep in his throat. "This wine tasting is for charity, or I wouldn't ask you to come. We've donated some of the wines, and it's good public relations for me to be there. If I were judging, you couldn't come with me. Judging is even more boring. You're shut up in a room with a few other people and all you do is sniff and taste, sniff and taste. And then you have to remember what you've sniffed and tasted, which is the hard part. You can't even talk to anyone else."

"How do you do it?"

"Keep from talking? That's easy. The other judges aren't that interesting."

"You really are a snob, aren't you?"

"Yes."

"I meant how do you remember what you've sniffed and tasted?"

"They never have more than about fifteen wines. And I take notes. Will you come with me Sunday?"

"I haven't even said I'd go Saturday."

"Will you accompany me to the theater Saturday night? And will you bring your book for me, the one you're writing?"

I hesitated, but knew what I was going to say. "Yes and maybe."

"Good. Now, what would you like to see?"

I gave him several choices—I hadn't been to the theater very much for the last couple of years, although I still read reviews. (Tom didn't like to go to the theater, I thought, and was surprised—not guilty, though—to realize how easy it was to forget about Tom.) The discussion of theater lasted through dinner, through coffee and brandy. Like the wine, the brandy was special. He told me about seeing *Phantom of the Opera* when it first opened in London. I envied him that, and fantasized for a moment going with him to London.

The ride back to Santa Clarissa was quiet, because I had to pay attention to the still unfamiliar road, and because it's hard to have a conversation in a sports car under the best of circumstances.

"Would you like to come in?" John asked, as I pulled up in front of the house.

"I don't think so," I answered. "Not tonight."

"All right. Although your honor would be safe. Francesca's presence has a dampening effect on lust. Besides, I have to go to Los Angeles later tonight."

"Tonight?"

"Yes. I have an early appointment tomorrow. Normally, I would have left hours ago, but I chose to have dinner with you instead. How long will you be staying in Santa Clarissa?"

"I'll drive back to Los Angeles sometime tomorrow, depending on what time I can see Phil Grademon."

"Are you going to ask him about Rick Clarence?"

"I might. I might nose around a little. How else will I find out whether you had a motive?"

He was amused. "You have a lovely nose, and I hope you'll be careful with it." He leaned over and kissed the nose under discussion, and then slid his mouth down over mine. His lips were warm, fleshy without being soft. Almost before I knew what was happening, I was responding to him, tongue to tongue. I broke the contact.

"This is getting dangerous," I whispered, leaning my head against his shoulder, aware of his muscles, aware of strength hidden by a well-cut jacket.

"I'd guess you like living dangerously."

"A little dangerously—but not too dangerously. And I need some time to assess how dangerous you are."

56

"I understand. I'll call you Saturday and let you know what time I'll be there." He kissed me again, just as persuasively, but not as urgently. And this time he pulled away. "Good night."

"Good night."

I turned the Alfa around and started back to the road, my face flushed and my hands barely steady on the steering wheel. And I almost hit a black Cadillac limousine on its way in. The Cadillac backed up clumsily, its headlights shooting dizzily around the house, until I had room to get out of the drive, then it pulled in again. I wanted to see who got out of the car, but the car was parked at an angle that blocked the path to the front door. Man or woman, I wondered. Not a romantic attachment—or certainly not one he had expected, because he had asked me in. Probably nothing more sinister than his ride to Los Angeles.

I was ready for bed when I reached the Mission Inn. And I missed my cats—especially Blaze, who slept curled up against the small of my back, almost like the pressure of another person in bed with me—but I dreamed of John's mouth.

I was still dreaming about him when I finally woke up. Damn.

I dressed in the same fuchsia jumpsuit, wished I had brought another change of clothes, breakfasted lightly at the same coffee shop where I had lunched the day before, and reached the Grademon Winery about ten-thirty. The tasting room was open (Grademon didn't have tours), and the same young man was behind the counter. It was early enough that he was sober. And clearly suffering from a hangover. His face was pinched and ashy, showing lines that weren't there the day before. All the blood in his face had flowed to his eyes and stayed there. Yesterday I would have placed him in his mid-twenties. Today he looked ten years older, and probably felt fifty. I could even see bits of gray in his dark shag of hair that I hadn't noticed before. His good looks weren't going to last long, and he wasn't going to age well.

"Today's wines are the same as yesterday's," he snapped peevishly.

"That's okay—I was looking not for wine, but for the winemaker. Is Phil here today?"

He looked as if it pained him to hear my voice. He nodded slightly and pointed to his left. "Through that door. Somewhere among the barrels."

"Thanks."

I entered a long, dimly lit room containing several rows of large oak barrels. The first aisle was empty, but halfway down the second aisle I saw a heavyset redheaded man who appeared to be plunging a large hypodermic needle through a cork in the top of one of the barrels.

"What are you doing?" I asked.

"What?"

I had startled him so much he almost dropped the syringe, or whatever it was.

"I'm sorry. I just wondered what you were adding to the wine."

"Oh. No. I'm not adding anything. I'm checking it. To see if it's ready to bottle."

We stared at each other. I was unnerved by the discovery of how easy it would be to poison a whole barrel of wine, if you knew what you were doing.

"I'm Morgan Reeves," I finally said, recovering. "I'm researching an article on wine for *Explore!* magazine. I gather you're Phil Grademon? Would you mind if I asked a few questions?"

He ignored my outstretched hand. "I'm not sure."

Phil Grademon was clad only in the ubiquitous khaki shorts, even though he had somehow missed out when God was passing out southern California beautiful bodies. His torso was lumpy, as if he sometimes exercised and sometimes ate too much, so the muscle and fat had to battle for position. The lumps were covered with white skin blotched with discolorations too large to be labeled freckles. His face was

58

pleasant enough, except for the unfortunate color of his skin and the watery blue of his eyes.

"How do you decide if the wine's ready to bottle?" I hoped I could recover from my lousy beginning.

"Color. Taste. That kind of thing."

He seemed off balance, uncomfortable with me there. The syringe was still poised, neither quite in nor quite out of the cork.

"Oh." Pause. "What happens next?"

"After the wine is bottled?"

"Well—then it's released, I guess." I answered my own question, feeling dumb.

"No. I hold it until it's ready."

"When is that?"

"It depends."

The tension was getting worse. He still hadn't moved. I wasn't doing this right. I changed the subject. "I understand you're also the winemaker at Novelli."

"Yes."

"Isn't that a tremendous lot of work—two wineries?"

"Sometimes."

"Have you always wanted to be a winemaker?"

"Yeah, I guess so."

"Oh?"

"Yeah."

"How did you become involved with the Novelli Winery?"

"Knew Eva at Davis."

"And she introduced you to her father?"

"Yeah."

"Tell me what it was like, starting the Novelli Winery."

"I didn't start it with them."

"I thought you were their first winemaker."

"No."

"Who was?"

"Henri Cheverin."

"When did you come into the picture?"

"A couple of years later."

I can't establish rapport with someone who looks past me. Phil Grademon was looking over my shoulder at the wall. I began to understand what John meant, when he doubted that Phil would be as self-disclosing.

"And starting this winery?"

"What?"

"What was it like to start your own winery?"

Phil finally removed the syringe from the cork. It was partly filled with a dark red liquid. He started down the aisle, and I followed.

"Had a lot of help."

"What are some of the things you've learned that they didn't teach you at Davis?"

"Just stuff I had to get through practice."

"Oh?"

Phil ignored the "oh."

"Tell me about Davis," I continued.

"Good school."

I was becoming impatient. This wasn't helping my article at all. If I threw in a question about the murder, that might get a rise out of him.

"I understand you knew Rick Clarence, the man murdered in the Novelli wine cellar, at Davis. What do you think happened?"

But I wasn't prepared for his reaction. He stopped and turned, once more staring over my shoulder. Tears started to flow from his soft blue eyes, down his mottled cheeks, splashing onto the floor in front of him. Dark wine leaked from the syringe held upright in his hand. Like blood.

"I don't know," he whispered.

"I'm sorry," I said, feeling like an insensitive fool. "I'm truly sorry. I thought you had barely kept in touch with him. I didn't know you cared so much."

"I loved him." The tears kept splashing.

"Is there anything I can do?"

"No."

I stood there trying to engage eyes that didn't want to meet mine. "Would you rather I left?"

"Yes."

"Would you mind if we talk again sometime, when this isn't so raw?"

"I don't know."

I was unnerved, watching him, his lumpy shoulders heaving.

"I'm really sorry. I didn't mean to do this. I'll leave now, and I hope I see you again under better circumstances."

He didn't say anything, and I left. I went straight to my car, gliding quickly through the tasting room. How could Will Baca possibly suspect Phil? You always kill the one you love?

The drive from Santa Clarissa to Los Angeles seemed longer than ever in the early afternoon heat. When I finally reached the house, I walked straight from the front door to the small porch off the kitchen that held my washer and dryer, stripped off my clothes, and dropped them in the washing machine.

Body and clothes attended to, I picked up the mail. I ripped open the envelope with the check first, even though I knew how small it was going to be. My telephone bill was staggering—had I really talked that long, to that many people? Thank God most of it was business. A Smithsonian catalogue I set aside to look at later. I loved to look at Smithsonian catalogues, which was doubtless why they sent me so many. I tossed out a copy of *Welcome to Our World,* a monthly magazine put out by one of the religious cults striving for respectability. I had done a book review for them once, over a year ago, and they had evidently decided to comp me for life. Much as I disapproved of their politics, I almost wished they would hire me to do something else. Almost.

I hadn't checked the messages on the machine yet, because I didn't really want to call anyone back. But I really couldn't keep putting it off. I poured a glass of mineral water, went into my tiny, overheated office, turned on the ceiling fan that I had recently installed, and flipped the answering machine to playback. Fred wanted me to call. Good, it was too late to call the East Coast today. I could call him in the morning. Elly Davis, a friend from my Los Angeles University days, was just checking in to see how I was. Elly was hard to get hold of. I would try during her office hours on Monday. And Tom called.

Did I have to call Tom back right now? No. I could work for a while first. I could start a file of notes for the article. I turned on the computer and created a file for Santa Clarissa Wines. The fan started to cool the office a little, and Chandra appeared from somewhere, hopping from the floor to my lap, and then onto the printer. For some reason she had decided that the printer was the place to sleep. It probably lay at a good angle from the fan.

I typed in everything I had learned, realizing it wasn't very much. I had clearly been distracted, first by the murder and then by John. I would see him on Saturday. Maybe Will would even have made his arrest by then. And it wouldn't be John, of course, or anyone close to him. I shoved that thought aside.

I worked until after six, coming up with a tentative outline, then decided it was time to stop writing about wine and start drinking it. And it was time to call Tom back.

He answered the phone on the second ring.

"Look, we really have to talk," he said. "Why don't you come back up here for the weekend?"

I paused, caught, guilty. "Because I have other plans for the weekend."

My guilt became worse in the silence. Finally, he broke it.

"When did you make other plans?"

"Yesterday."

"God damn it, did you get suckered in by John Novelli? That guy is the biggest womanizer in the state. I thought you were more together than that."

"Listen, I've never made any promises to you, you know that." That was a terrible thing to say. If I didn't get out of this relationship soon—or let Tom know I was already out—I wasn't going to like myself very much. "I'm sorry. But I don't

62

want anybody to get possessive of me. And I don't feel like being put down right now."

"I'm sorry. But it is Novelli, isn't it?"

It took me a while to say it. "Yes."

Another silence. He broke it.

"Why don't you call me when you're ready to talk?"

"Okay." The silences were getting longer and longer. "Tom?"

"Yeah?"

"I just realized that you really do love me."

"If I didn't, I'd find you a lot easier to handle."

"I'm sorry. I don't know what to do with that."

"I know. I'm sorry, too."

That was all there was to say.

I was applying a last coat of mascara to my left eyelashes when Bubba and Blaze thundered down the hall and collided in the doorway to the bedroom, both heading for the open window. They were my early warning system. Within seconds, the doorbell rang.

John was prompt. When he called, he had said seven o'clock, and it was only a couple of minutes after—and my house was hard to find. He had suggested that we eat after the show, and I had countered with the suggestion that he arrive in time for a glass of wine and an appetizer.

I had dashed out to pick up sourdough bread, crab, Brie, and a dry California champagne—there was no way I was going to risk choosing a Chardonnay for him.

I had also polished a couple of pieces of family silver, including the champagne bucket, arranged the food, and covered it with plastic. The cats—all four of them—loved crab. And I rinsed and dried my two good champagne flutes. It annoyed me that they had been sitting unused so long that they were dusty.

I vacuumed the sofa free of cat fur. And the porch—I remembered to sweep the peahen shit off the porch.

John was wearing an open-necked white shirt, a sport jacket, and slacks, somehow managing to look so elegant that I was a bit intimidated, almost afraid to touch him. I was glad I was wearing a dress, a white dress with fringe and a matching fringed shawl. My high-heeled white sandals made me just a little taller than he.

He solved the intimidation problem by touching my cheek, leaning forward and kissing me lightly on the side of the mouth.

"You look stunning," he said. "Like a model. I must tell you, I've been looking forward to seeing you again from the moment you left."

"Good," I replied. "I've been looking forward to seeing you, too." There was an awkward moment, and then I continued. "Let me get the wine."

"Is there something I can do to help?"

"Yes, of course. You can save me a trip."

He popped the champagne cork and carried the bucket and the glasses into the living room. I followed with the food and plates. He filled the glasses and handed me one.

"To the gods," he said, clicking his glass against mine.

If we were truly drinking to the gods, we should probably have poured a little onto my ugly red carpet, in lieu of earth, but we didn't. And he said it as if he meant us.

"To the gods," I answered, and drank with him. Breaking contact with his eyes, I tore off a piece of bread, heaped the carefully seasoned crab on it and handed it to him. "Here. We probably ought to eat something, so we won't be late."

He took a bite. "This is terrific," he mumbled with his mouth full.

"Thank you. I'm glad you like it."

I broke off another hunk of bread and piled crab on it. He was right, it was terrific.

Marcia jumped from somewhere onto the end table next to John and screamed.

"A cat," he said coolly. "You have a cat."

"Cats," I said brightly, ignoring his tone. "I have four of them, but the two males won't come in the living room while you're here. They don't like strangers, and they think everyone but me is a stranger. I'm surprised Chandra isn't around, though."

"Oh. Is there some way you could discourage this one from being in the living room while I'm here?"

"Yes, I can put her out. I'm sorry you don't like cats."

"Actually, I'm allergic to them." He was sitting stiffly, as if he didn't want to expose too much of his clothing to the possibility of cat fur on the couch. "Do you have a decongestant I can take before the attack hits?"

"Of course." I got the pills from the bathroom cabinet and was just in time to close the bedroom window on an indignant Marcia. The cat's scream was muted by the glass. She wanted her share of the crab.

Chandra had shown up from somewhere and was rubbing her body against the coffee table, tail waving perilously close to the food, when I returned. John was still sitting stiffly. I handed him the pills and grabbed Chandra, who protested.

"Sorry," I said as I dumped Chandra on the porch. "There won't be any more of them."

"It's all right," John replied, visibly relaxing as he took the decongestant. "In fact, I'm sorry. It must be a nuisance for you to have a guest who's allergic to cats. After all, they live here."

"Well, it's a nuisance for them, but they'll survive. It means I have to shut the door, though, or they'll come back in. I hope you'll be okay with just the fan."

"I'll be okay," he said. His good humor was returning.

"Good." I took the seat next to him once again and piled crab on another hunk of bread. "How was your week?"

"Difficult," he said soberly.

"Because of what happened Tuesday?"

66

"More than that. Will Baca's dead."

"Oh, God, I'm sorry. How did it happen?"

"Nobody's quite sure yet. Apparently his car went off the road, overturned, and hit a tree. A couple of campers found him yesterday morning."

"Then it happened Thursday night?"

"Yes. The deputy got worried when he didn't show up Friday morning and tried his house. Before he could do anything more than that, the campers called in."

"Does anybody know what he was doing? Was the place where he was found on his way anywhere?"

"I suppose so is the answer to your first question, and of course is the answer to your second. Why are you asking?"

"Well—Will's lived in that area all his life, right?"

"More or less."

"Did he drink or do hard drugs?"

"Not that I'm aware."

"So I was wondering if maybe it wasn't an accident."

John was amused. "I realize there's a coincidence here. Deputy investigating a murder dies in accident. But it was an accident. Some sort of mechanical problem, I don't remember what. Those things happen, you know. Unfortunately."

"I know, but it seems so strange that it would happen now. Had he made an arrest yet?"

"What do you mean?"

"I thought he would find the murderer fairly easily. Santa Clarissa is a small town—there couldn't have been too many suspects. That's all."

John sat there for a moment, watching me thoughtfully.

"No arrest," he said finally.

I bristled, feeling challenged, not certain why. "Who lives in that area?"

"He was found on the other side of Los Robles, heading north. Of course people live there—he was just past the Lindale Winery."

"Could anyone at Lindale have been connected with Rick Clarence?"

"I don't know. I think you're grasping at straws, though, trying to connect Will's accident with Clarence's murder." He was still cool.

"Maybe." More likely not. "I know you had problems with Will, and I'd guess they have to do with Eva and the failed marriage. How do you feel now?"

John sighed. "Sorry. I liked Will, I really did. He is, after all, the father of my grandson. And I may have blamed him for things he couldn't help. Things that weren't his fault, or at least were as much Eva's as his. In any case, I'm sorry he's dead."

I took his hand, impulsively. "How has Eva reacted?"

"She seems all right, but Johnny is devastated. He adored his father. He never understood why his parents didn't live together."

"How old is he?"

"He's twelve now, but he was only two when Eva and Will separated."

I tried once more. "Don't you have any reservations about calling what happened to Will an accident?"

"None. Morgan, my dear, it was an accident. If Will had indeed solved Rick Clarence's murder, someone else will, too, in time. And, Morgan, once and for all, I do not believe that the murderer is someone close to my house."

He said "house" as if it had some kind of classical strength behind it, like the House of Atreus, or the House of Cadmus. I wondered if his house was equally doomed, or if the god from the machine would somehow arrive to save what was left of John's family.

With a clear effort, he smiled, turning his attention to me, and refilled our wine glasses.

"That's enough about Will," he said.

"Do you really want to go to the theater tonight?"

"Yes, I do. I rarely go to the smaller houses, and you made an interesting choice."

"I gave you several choices."

"I know, all interesting. Anyway, I am a selfish man, and I

am unwilling to give up the evening—I refuse to consider giving up the evening because my former son-in-law met with an accident."

"Okay." I picked up my glass. "To the evening, then."

"Yes," he replied, not clicking his glass against mine as much as caressing it. "To the evening."

But we couldn't really get a conversation going, and fortunately it was soon time to leave. Even with the fan, I was feeling damp and sticky from the heat. I carried my shawl over my arm, knowing I'd need it later. The weather was now more typical of August in L.A.—the heat wave had broken to the extent that it was cooling off at night.

A black Cadillac limo was parked in front of Norman's house. I guessed it was the one I had seen coming in as I left the other night. As we started down the front steps, a chauffeur came around to open the door.

"Has he been waiting down here the whole time?" I asked.

"Of course. That's his job. Besides, he was probably more comfortable than we were. The car's air conditioned."

He introduced me to the chauffeur, Derek, who looked like a bodyguard, tall and bulky and flat-faced. I wondered why John would need a bodyguard, and how long Derek had been with him, but held my questions.

The theater was a converted movie house on Sunset Boulevard, very Art Deco with liver-colored carpets and walls and crystal sconces. The ceiling of the auditorium sported a faded pastoral orgy, fauns and nymphs and satyrs cavorting. The play seemed appropriate—a musical satire on the fifties. By the time it ended, the weather had indeed cooled to the point where a shawl was needed.

"Those were the good old days," John sighed as we left the theater.

"The fifties? The fifties were the good old days?"

"Of course. The economy was expanding, business was booming, we felt in control of our destiny in a way that we haven't since."

"White men felt in control of their destinies, you mean."

69

"Yes, I suppose I do mean that. You wouldn't see the fifties as the good old days, would you?"

"No, I wouldn't."

"What would you like to eat?"

"Pizza? That was very fifties."

"Pizza it is."

Derek drove us to a chrome and glass pizza parlor with a lot of mirrors on the walls, where we agreed to split a Caesar salad and a small pizza with smoked chicken, sun-dried tomatoes, and feta cheese—not very fifties after all.

"As a professional taster, how would you describe it?" I asked, when the waiter had poured the wine.

"This? I'd describe it as *pour la soif*, a wine to drink because we're thirsty. But it has some character, it's clean, fragrant, grassy. You should learn more about wine, since you like to drink it so much."

"I've thought about taking a class. I haven't done so simply because I can't afford the wine habit I have now, and developing a taste for better wine would only make the situation worse."

"That's true. But then you simply have to find a way to afford it. If you want something badly enough, you'll find a way to pay for it."

"How have you paid for what you have? What business were you in here in Los Angeles?"

"Actually, I'm still in business in Los Angeles. I have a variety of interests, mostly in real estate and agriculture."

"Agriculture? Other than grapes?"

"Yes. But my involvement is purely financial, other than wine."

The waiter brought the salad, with an extra plate. I set about splitting it.

"Caesar salads aren't as much fun when they aren't mixed right at the table," I commented as I gave John a plate.

"They're not as good, either, but pizza parlors—even California pizza establishments—aren't usually noted for the excellence of their Caesar salads."

70

"We could have ordered a different salad."

"We could have, but we both seemed to want this one. And it really isn't bad," he added as he took a large bite.

I liked watching his sensual enjoyment of the food. I took a smaller bite.

"Too much cheese," I commented. "And do you suppose that anyone actually coddles the egg for Caesar salad any more?"

"I'm certain there are restaurants where they do, but don't ask me to name one."

"How about the Hotel Caesar in Tijuana?"

"I'll take you there sometime. We'll order one and ask them."

I was caught once again by the intensity of his blue eyes. "Just as long as you don't suggest a bullfight," I said, as lightly as I could manage.

"I've never enjoyed bloodshed."

"Does that have something to do with your having a body-guard?"

"What? You mean Derek?" He started to chuckle, almost choking on his salad. "I suppose he does look like one, doesn't he?"

"What is he?"

John took a moment to swallow his bite of salad. "I'm afraid he's nothing exciting or mysterious. He's simply a rather large man without any particular skills or talents except loyalty who drives me around and runs errands from time to time."

"What kind of errands?"

"He doesn't kill people for me, if that's what you're asking."

"Not really. He doesn't look like the type who would poison someone in the wine cellar. But he's awfully formidable for a chauffeur."

"I know. That's one reason I like having him around."

"But why would you need someone formidable?"

He shrugged, and was saved from an immediate answer by the arrival of the waiter with the pizza.

"I really don't," he said. "Here, let me help you."

He neatly separated two very messy slices of pizza from the circle and transferred them to the small plates.

"Thank you. Why is it that I get the feeling there's a lot more to you than you're telling me?"

"Because there is, of course. I'm willing to tell you anything you want to know about me—I told you that when we first met—and I also told you there's a lot to know. I hired Derek in the sixties, when there was a lot of unrest, and I wanted someone to drive the girls back and forth to school, and to be there in the house when I was gone."

"You mean he's been with you for twenty years?"

"More than that."

"That's amazing. But why were you so worried? You didn't live in Watts."

"In case you've forgotten, the problems of the sixties weren't limited to the cities."

"Of course. You said some of your interests were in agriculture, didn't you? You were one of the bad guys—one of the ones we stopped eating grapes and lettuce because of."

"Not directly. But I had investments in those areas. And it seemed to me that wherever I went, there was the potential for violence. I wanted my family safe. I was lucky to have found Derek—I think he would have given up his life for my daughters. Probably for my wife, too, at the time."

"Sort of like a big German shepherd."

"I suppose you could say that, although I've never thought of him that way."

"How do you think of him? And how do you think of the Chicanos who work in your fields?"

John sighed. "I feel a great sense of responsibility toward Derek."

"Noblesse oblige?"

"Are you always this testy?"

"I don't think so. I'd back off if I thought you really might take offense."

"You're right. I'm not offended. And I'm not embarrassed

to admit that that's part of it. Derek will work for me as long as I'm alive, or as long as he's able. I'll see that he's taken care of if he's sick or hurt, and I've provided for him in my will. As far as the field workers are concerned, I don't know what to say. In the fields I'm directly concerned with—the ones at the winery—the grapes are picked by machine. The gleaning is done by hand, of course, but those workers belong to someone else."

" 'Belong' to someone else?"

"Yes. I work within the system. I'm not really interested in reforming it—I've done too well living by its rules. And they're not really bad rules. You might say that I've freed my own slaves, but that I'm not ready to fight a civil war over someone else's right to keep them."

"How can you say the rules are good, when they don't even require you to provide sanitary facilities for the field workers?"

"I don't approve of that, of course, but I'm not going to take up the cause. I have too little to gain and too much to lose. And by the way, don't make the mistake of confusing the rules with the laws."

"Are you telling me you haven't always stayed within the laws?"

"I wouldn't dream of telling you that. Would you like coffee?"

I grimaced. "Yes, I would. Decaf."

"What are you thinking?"

"I'm wondering why I'm attracted so often to men whose values are so different from mine."

"Perhaps because you like to argue. Perhaps because it gives you an excuse to walk away."

"You would have made a good therapist."

"I would have. But it wasn't a life I wanted. While we're on the subject of you, however, why didn't you bring your manuscript?"

"Quite honestly, I forgot when you told me about Will. And

I printed out a copy for you, too. You can get it when you take me home."

"I'd hoped I wouldn't have to take you home quite yet. Are you tired? Bored?"

"Neither."

"Then why don't we skip coffee here. We can have coffee—decaf, if you will—and brandy at my place."

"Your place?"

"Yes. I keep an apartment here in Los Angeles. And going back to your place is out of the question."

I started to bristle, but decided that with the cats and the heat, he was right. "Okay" was all I said.

The apartment turned out to be a penthouse in a Santa Monica high-rise with a panoramic view of the night sky and the ocean. The living room was large enough that the grand piano took only one corner of it, safely out of range of the wall of windows. The only other furnishings were a massive white conversational group around a marble table in front of a fireplace. And his art collection—all properly lighted.

"My God," I said, stopping short as I entered the room. "I don't know where to start."

"Where would you like to start?"

I walked toward the closest one. "Tell me about this one."

"First, tell me what you see."

"I see a very stylized and bloody Christ on the cross with a crown of thorns, with a tiny thief on either side. Somebody's private version of hell. And I wonder why you'd want to live with it."

"Interesting. Some people see a Mexican straw figure and two wine glasses. I see a great deal of compassion and humor and honesty. With some splotches of red paint. I don't find living with that a problem. Nor do I consider 'livability' a necessary criterion for buying a piece. I'm not here that much. This particular artist has turned out to be a rather good investment."

"I think I don't want to play this game."

"No one said you had to."

74

"Do you play the piano? I didn't see one in Santa Clarissa."

"I do play, and I don't have one there. I suppose I should."

"Should?"

"No one else in the family plays, and I rarely play for other people these days, but I do wish sometimes I had one available."

"Why don't you play for people? Will you play for me?"

"I play only under certain circumstances, and that house is simply too public. And of course I'll play for you. But first, what would you like with your coffee?"

"How about Kahlua and cream?"

"You really want that *in* your coffee."

"Yes."

"Let me tell Derek. He'll fix you something special."

"So he does have talents other than loyalty?"

"A few learned skills."

John disappeared for a moment, and went straight to the piano when he returned. I had expected Bach or Mozart—definitely something classical. But the first few chords were clearly jazz. And then he started to sing, with a rich, full baritone voice.

He had an easy style, mellow, soft, seductive. I moved next to the piano, wanting to be closer as he sang. As he finished the last chords of "That's All," Derek brought our coffee. Mine was in a glass mug with whipped cream on top. His was in a cup, accompanied by a brandy snifter.

When Derek left, I said, "You don't mean that."

"What?"

"The line about only giving me love that lasts forever. You don't mean that."

"Of course not. But then, you don't want that."

"You're tough, you know."

I was feeling a bit manipulated, and I didn't want that, either.

"So are you. I know you're vulnerable, but you're tough at the same time. That's part of what intrigues me so much about you."

And then I didn't feel manipulated any more. I was caught by his eyes, I wanted to be caught by his eyes.

"More. Sing to me more."

He smiled slightly, and nodded. He started to play, and his hands and his eyes and his voice told me that I was his whole world. A second glass mug appeared at my side just as I was finishing the first. The coffee was warm and rich and mellow and very alcoholic. I had started out standing beside the piano, then I was leaning against it, then sitting beside him. As his hands held the final chord of "But Beautiful," he leaned over and kissed me, the same urgent kiss that he had first given me in the car. I opened my mouth. This time I didn't pull away.

"Would you like to move someplace more comfortable?" he whispered so close to my ear that I barely heard it.

"I think so," I said. "I think I'd like that."

"This way then," he said, gently pushing me off the piano bench, walking with his arm softly across my shoulders.

The bedroom shared a wall, and a fireplace, with the living room. The window facing the ocean was an extension of that same living room wall. That, and the large white bed, were all I saw. He started to kiss me again, and we fell onto the bed, not quite losing contact, undressing each other as we dropped and rolled. The smell of his body, the film of perspiration in the heat, the breeze from the ocean through the open window, the faint scent of flowers on the table beside the bed, filled my head. The softness of his skin, the definition, the unexpected strength of his muscles. Wet, we were both wet. And I loved him.

It was almost impossible to fall asleep next to him—I kept wanting to kiss him, wanting more long after my body was exhausted, after his was exhausted. When I did sleep, it was sound and dreamless. I woke once in the night, stumbling around searching for a bathroom, not sure where I was, delighted when I realized, and then woke again with the gray light and a slight breeze coming in from the windows, cool and comfortable. Santa Monica penthouses may be the only places in L.A. that don't need air conditioning. John woke shortly thereafter and reached for me, pulled me toward him.

Derek arrived later, dressed in white cotton shirt and pants, carrying a tray with a thermos of fresh coffee and two mugs. He filled the two mugs as we relaxed, nuzzled each other. John thanked him and he left. I was pleasantly surprised to note that there was cream on the tray. I was also surprised at my lack of embarrassment in front of Derek. He had obviously performed this ritual often—it was clearly one of the errands he ran for John. Bring coffee, and don't make whoever-she-is uncomfortable when you do.

"How are you?" John asked.

"I'm fine. But I should have warned you—I'm not very good at mornings."

"Nonsense. You're terrific at mornings."

"That's not what I meant. I'm a little slow to get going, so you'll have to carry the conversation."

"Then there won't be any. I want to run on the beach anyway—I'll be gone for about half an hour—you can go back to sleep, or if you'd like, I'll have Derek bring you the papers."

"Papers?"

"Yes. I have both *Times.*"

"Oh, dear God, this is truly heaven. You have the Sunday *New York Times* magazine. I can't tell you how much I've missed William Safire and the crossword puzzle."

"William Safire?"

"Yes. You probably only read his other columns, but his ones on words are wonderful."

"That's right—you're a writer. But why have you missed them? Why not have them every Sunday?"

I hesitated. "Someone used to save them for me. Years ago. And it always seemed silly to have my own subscription just for the crossword puzzles."

"Would you like me to save them for you?"

"Yes, I think I would," I whispered.

"I'll be back before you have the puzzle done," he said, kissing me lightly. "Don't move more than necessary."

"I won't, but I bet I have the puzzle done before you're back."

"Don't, because you can't win. I'll simply cut my run short."

"Would you really do that?"

"I would."

"Winning means that much to you?"

"Yes."

I was half-propped with pillows, and he had rolled over to face me. I studied the tanned, lined face, the amazing blue eyes with their dark brows. I knew he meant it. And the knowledge chilled me a little. What else would he do to win? I leaned over and kissed his cheek.

"I'm sorry," I said.

I watched his body as he headed for the bathroom, coffee cup in hand. Whoever he was, he was comfortable in his own skin. And it was indeed beautiful skin. I didn't want to think it might be murderer's skin.

Derek reappeared shortly with the papers.

"Derek?" I asked hesitantly. "Do you think you could find my handbag?"

John could have won the bet simply by depriving me of my glasses and a pen. I was wondering about a bathrobe, when a piece of pale blue silk floated down on top of me.

"In case you feel absolutely compelled to move while I'm gone," he said.

"Thank you. I wasn't looking forward to doing the puzzle scrunched up—and I was thinking about using the bathroom."

I wondered whose bathrobe I was wearing. Actually, it was safely androgynous—it might even have been John's. I sniffed it carefully, but it had been washed since last worn. I slid into it, liking the soft fabric, wanting, like a cat, to imbue it with my own scent, wanting him to recognize that scent when he picked up the robe.

When he returned from his run, I had finished the cross-word and was playing with the acrostic. We ignored each other while he did a few cooling-off exercises on the floor. There was a little softness around his belly, but he clearly took pride in his condition.

"What would you like to do?" he asked as he wiped off the sweat with a towel. "I have to be at the wine tasting at two, and I'd like you to come with me. We could have breakfast now, and after that you can stay as long as you like, although I have some phone calls to make and a few other things to dispose of, so you'll have to amuse yourself. If you want to go home, Derek can drive you. The wine tasting is at the Bilt-more, so I could pick you up about twenty before two."

"I do want to go with you," I replied. "And I'll stay for breakfast, but I'd rather amuse myself at home."

"Whatever you like."

I wondered if Derek cooked, but I didn't find out. Breakfast turned out to be a plate of fresh fruit—strawberries, kiwis, cantaloupe, pineapple, oranges—and a plate of assorted pastries served at a small glass table on the balcony. I hadn't realized it the night before, but the balcony was large enough for a good-size cocktail party. It didn't look as if he thought in terms of large groups, however. Besides the small table and chairs where we sat, the only other furniture was a pair of chaises longues. There were a number of pots with showy, flowering portulaca, out toward the edge where they could have sun all day, and potted greenery closer to the house. But I had a sense that we were private, isolated—there were only the two of us, the bare balcony, and the ocean, all grays and pale blues and whites, except for the fruit and the flowers, like a scene from a surreal French film.

I felt grungy amid the opulence, wishing I had thought to bring a toothbrush and some face cream, even a pair of jeans so I wouldn't have to put my sweaty dress back on.

John had apparently meant it when he said that if I didn't talk, there wouldn't be any conversation. Although making sure my needs were met, he was otherwise engrossed in *The New York Times* business section.

Derek was equally silent when he drove me home. For once, I was glad to hear Marcia scream.

I wasn't sure what one wore to an afternoon wine tasting at the Biltmore, but was fairly certain that John wouldn't be wearing a tie. I decided on a silky, cream-colored jumpsuit that I could dress up with some chunky gold jewelry and a scarf.

Whenever I agonized over what to wear, I thought of my mother, who had spent a fortune on clothes, who always had the right thing to wear. I could remember her telling me (was I nine or ten at the time?) that I would not grow up to be the kind of woman who looked the same all the time, that I would look either better than most or worse than most, but I wouldn't look ordinary.

Probably it was a mother-fulfilling prophecy, but maintenance has always been a problem for me. And while my mother was right, that I could look either terrific or terrible, she had somehow expected me to have control over the process, something I never gained, although I became better at it after she died.

There were times when I accepted my mother's curse joyfully, when I sailed into a room, knowing Ava Gardner couldn't have made a better entrance. And there were times when I put my heart and soul and a couple of hours in front of the mirror into looking great, and started out smashing, but then caught a glimpse of myself later, only to see limp hair and smeared mascara, or a spot of butter on my blouse.

And then there were the other days, when I knew before I left the house that it was a lost cause, that my mother's soul was sighing somewhere.

My perspective had tilted just a little, finally, when I was thirty-three and she was long dead, and I had seen my picture in a magazine with an article I had written. The photo had chilled me. I said to a friend, "I look just like my mother." My friend had responded, "Your mother must have been a pretty woman." "No," I said, "she wasn't. That's the point. I just realized this moment that she could have been and didn't know how."

Odd, how many women who only come into their own after their mothers die, who only then can stop worrying what their mothers would think of their clothes, of their men.

What would my mother have thought of John? She would have "seen right through him." "Don't get trapped by physical things," my mother would have snapped.

Yes ma'am. I hear you. And I don't plan on getting trapped by anything else, either.

Despite the film of sweat that formed on my skin immediately after the shower, and the knowledge that my hair would probably be limp with the heat about five minutes after we hit the Biltmore, I looked smashing when John arrived at precisely twenty before two.

I had the manuscript for my book in my hand when I opened the door. And I was dazzled all over again—the sun on his hair.

"I'm glad you decided to come with me," he said.

"Me too. Here."

"Thank you," he said, kissing me again. "And what is that peahen doing on your porch?"

"She hangs out with me," I said, a little embarrassed. "I hope you're not allergic to peahens, too."

"Not that I know of." He tucked the book under his arm, and held my hand all the way down the steps to the car.

I was slightly daunted, walking into the Grand Ballroom of the newly refurbished Biltmore on his arm, into a crowd of fifteen hundred people, all of whom seemed to know him. The Biltmore is an "old money" hotel—thick carpets, high ceilings, heavy pillars, subdued colors, and lots of mirrors with frames. But the crowd was mixed, all the way from stately gentlemen in white three-piece suits (barely sweating) to teenies in denim and glitter. I felt okay about what I was wearing.

The problem was that even with air conditioning, it was

warm, and there was so much wine to drink. John, I noticed, wasn't drinking. He walked around with a glass, but there was never anything in it. I was fascinated, though, wanting to try everything, all the Chardonnays and the champagnes and the Fumés Blancs (not the reds, I didn't want a headache, too many histamines in the reds, and I wouldn't risk an indelible spot on the jumpsuit), and all the shrimp and the pâté and the cheese, so at some point I left him and began wandering about the room on my own.

After tasting the first few wines, I was not only having trouble remembering them, I was having trouble telling them apart. Some were still better than others—some were so tart that I dumped them in the small bucket provided for that purpose. But most were in a vast middle range, drinkable, in fact definitely better than my usual house wine, but not terrific. At the end of three hours, it was all a bit hazy, and I hoped I was still making sense when I talked to people.

One of the people was Alida Cahill, who greeted me rather coolly. Again, I had a sense that Alida had been drinking, and that Alida held it well. And again I wondered whether it was Alida or John who had lied about the affair, and why she had brought it up at all, when she could simply have avoided the subject.

I wondered how many other women who were there, women he was introducing me to, that John had slept with. I was certain of at least two, from the way they looked at me.

Derek was, of course, waiting at the door with the Cadillac when we left the hotel.

"What would you like now?" John asked. "Would you like dinner? Would you like to come back to the beach with me?"

"No," I sighed. "I've eaten too much cheese and pâté and bread, so I don't want dinner. And I'm afraid I'm too drunk and too sleepy to be good company. Besides, I have to get up early tomorrow, and I'd rather be at home. I'm going back up to Santa Clarissa."

"Oh?"

"Yes. I have a lot more to do up there. I don't know nearly

enough. Besides, I'm still bothered by Will's so-called accident. I really am. I want to make sure somebody's taking it seriously. And then I think I may drive on up to Davis, talk to a couple of professors, get some background information for the article. But can we stay in touch? Can I call you when I get back?"

"Of course." He gave me private telephone numbers for both L.A. and Santa Clarissa. "I can't always call back immediately, but I promise I will within a day or two. And I'll read your manuscript."

"Oh, God," I groaned. "Leave a message, will you? Don't make me wait until I see you again."

"Soon," he said, cuddling me against his shoulder. "I'll see you soon."

When he left, I thought fleetingly that it might have been nice to spend another night at the beach. But it was also good to be home. I didn't like spending too many nights away from the cats. I hadn't quite finished the acrostic. I wanted to add just a few notes to my Santa Clarissa wine files. And a small voice in my head was telling me not to rush into anything with John Novelli.

Monday morning was seasonably warm, but the heat wave had definitely broken. I took my time with the paper—the Monday morning *Times* was thin, as usual—packed, left a message for Norman to feed the cats and Salome, and left a message for Elly at L.A. University. I was still on the road by eleven, and pulled into the parking lot behind the small building that held what had been Will Baca's office and the local jail around one-thirty.

The door was locked. Terrific, I thought. What could I do that would be useful while I waited? Lunch, at the little coffee shop. I decided to walk the few blocks. I almost walked into Alida Cahill, who was coming out of a small grocery store with a large bag of groceries. Alida was puffy-eyed, but apparently sober.

"I'm sorry," I said.

Alida looked at me. "Are you? For what?"

"For almost bumping into you. And for not having more of

a chance to talk at the wine tasting yesterday," I added in what I hoped was a conciliatory manner. "I was just about to have lunch. Would you like to join me?"

"I don't think so," Alida said, and then added politely, "but thank you for asking."

"Do you know by any chance when somebody is going to be in the sheriff's office?"

"No, why?"

"Well, because I wanted to talk with somebody, that's all. I heard about Will Baca's accident."

"Oh."

"And it bothered me," I blurted.

We stood eye to eye for a moment, like two cats testing, wary. The contact was broken as the young man from the Grademon Winery burst out of the grocery store and brushed me as he headed for a Jeep at the curb.

"Excuse me," he snipped as he passed.

"Of course," I said. "I guess we're blocking the door."

But he was gone.

"Rude bastards," Alida said.

I was startled. The expression seemed a bit crude, not what I would have expected from the carefully put-together Alida.

"What do you mean?"

"Both of them. I think I told you before that winemakers are an unsociable lot, but on the whole we're at least polite to one another. We recognize that there's a community of interest here, even if we don't always agree on what it is. They won't even join the Winemakers' Association."

"Maybe they feel they wouldn't be welcome."

"We're fairly tolerant of any dues-paying member," Alida said dryly, "no matter what they do when they aren't making wine."

"Is anybody up here happily married?"

"Is anybody anywhere happily married? There are one or two couples—you probably met the Lindales yesterday, they donated wine, too—"

I vaguely remembered a distinguished man with a well-trimmed gray beard and a bubbly blond wife half his age. I knew the name, however. It was at least third-generation California wealth, and the label on some good wines.

"—and Ernie and Cindy Frawn. They keep their own winery alive by working for everyone else. Cindy keeps the books for just about everybody in the valley, and Ernie helps out a lot, whatever people need."

"I don't know the name. What's the label?"

"Polarity Wines."

"I still don't know the name."

"I'm not surprised. Their wine is passable, but they don't make a lot of it, and they can't sell it for as much as they would need to."

"Probably I ought to talk with them."

"Probably you should."

"Thanks."

Alida nodded and left. I walked on to the coffee shop, wishing I'd thought to ask what the man's name was, the one from the Grademon tasting room.

After lunch, I walked back to the sheriff's office. Jerry Harris was there, sitting at Will's desk. He looked too small for the chair. He didn't remember meeting me at the winery, but he was eager to talk to somebody about Will.

"Awful, you know? Seeing him like that. Wheel must've snapped off on a curve, couldn't control the car. Found the wheel about a quarter of a mile away. Guy who looked at the car said the bearings froze, no fluid, happens sometimes in older cars, he said. Car flipped, landed upside down, skidded into a tree. Must've been fast, that's the only good thing. Funny, though, 'cause Will really took care of that car. Wouldn't think it'd have a problem like that."

"Could someone have tampered with it?" I asked.

"Why? Who'd want to do a thing like that?" Jerry got even smaller.

"I just wondered if it were possible."

"Something like that's always possible, I guess, but nobody'd want to hurt Will."

86

"Do you know where he was going?"

"Not for sure. He'd said something about how he might have to go to Davis, that there was some professor he wanted to talk to. It was about the dead man, the guy who was found in the Novelli Winery."

"Had he talked to you about that?"

"No, not really. I got called away on kind of a personal emergency the afternoon the corpse was discovered, and I didn't get back till Friday morning. I was real surprised when Will wasn't here."

"I'm sure you were. What are you going to do now?"

He slid farther down in the chair. If I asked him any more questions, Jerry Harris was going to become the invisible man.

"I don't know. Probably somebody'll come up from Santa Barbara in a day or two, and maybe he'll be able to figure it all out. And Novelli ain't gonna go nowhere."

"What do you mean?"

I had to ask him that one.

"Well, it has to be him, don't it? The guy died in his wine cellar, Grademon was out of town, and it sure wasn't one of the girls, or the old man. Who else could it be?"

Who else indeed? I shut my eyes for a moment. I had to think about this. When I opened them again, Harris was staring out the window.

"Is there any evidence that he was meeting John that night?"

"What?"

"Did Rick Clarence have a calendar, an appointment book, anything that would indicate he was planning to meet John?"

"I don't know, I haven't looked through his stuff. Will probably did, but I haven't. I've just been too busy since I got back, here all alone."

"Are his things here?"

"Yeah, nobody's picked them up. His clothes are in the closet over there, and his personal stuff is in the file drawer."

He pointed first to an unfinished pine wardrobe, then to a four-drawer steel file.

"Why don't we take a look—see if we can figure out what Clarence was doing when he was murdered?"

"You're right, I probably ought to see what's there— should've done it first thing—but I can't let you go through it, I'm sorry."

"Okay. You look."

I stood in front of the desk and waited. Jerry frowned, probably trying to figure out a way to get rid of me without checking the file. Finally, he gave in. He got a key from the center drawer of the desk and unlocked the file cabinet. I followed at what I hoped was a discreet distance and peered over his shoulder.

In the bottom drawer of the file cabinet was a plastic gar-bage bag containing sundry toilet articles, a watch, a wallet, and one of those big, life-planning appointment books. Jerry picked it up and returned to the desk. He unceremoniously ripped the Velcro tabs, thumbed through a few pages, and stopped.

"Well, that's no good," he said.

"What do you mean?"

"The pages aren't there. About two weeks missing, that's what I mean."

"Where? Let me see."

I grabbed the book. He was right. Several pages, including the night of the murder, had been torn out.

"How did that happen?" I asked.

"I didn't do it," Jerry said, hearing the accusation in my tone, "and I don't know who did. Nobody had access to the file, I swear it. The guy must of done it himself, before he was offed."

"What about fingerprints? Did you check for fingerprints?"

"Oh, hell, lady, you can't get fingerprints off this textured stuff. Forget that. Besides, we've touched it, smeared any-thing that might have been there."

I thought about yelling at him, wavered, then backed off.

"Well, why don't we look through the rest of his things, maybe there's something else that would help."

"Nah. I shouldn't even have done this, with you here. But it was a good idea, it might have helped. And no harm, since the pages are missing."

"Right."

Shit.

What now? How could I prove—to myself, anyway—that John didn't do it? I thought about touching him, about how much I wanted to see him again. I had to know he wasn't a murderer.

I left the sheriff's office and walked back to the telephone booth at the gas station, the only one I had seen. I sat down on the phone booth seat to look at the directory. The station attendant, the same dirty youth in coveralls and a cap who had directed me to a restaurant, stared at me for a moment and then returned to his spot in the shade.

The listing was under Eva Novelli. Circlecross Ranch, Buellton. I dialed the number, betting I knew what the brand looked like.

When I asked the throaty female voice that answered the phone if Eva was there, the reply was, "No, she's at her office."

I rummaged for an old envelope in my handbag and wrote down the number she gave me. This time I reached an answering machine.

"This is Eva Novelli. At the sound of the beep, leave as long a message as you like. I am the only person who will hear the message. I check this machine frequently, and I will call you back as soon as I can. If this is an emergency, call 555-1403 and ask them to page me. I will call you back immediately."

I explained to the machine who I was and why I could not be reached at the moment. I said I would try again later. Eva Novelli, feminist therapist.

I left the telephone booth and looked for a place to sit. I didn't see one, so I started walking back toward my car. This was nuts. The whole idea was nuts. Jerry Harris was right—

somebody from Santa Barbara would come up here and figure it all out. And murder investigations were for professionals. However curious I was. However much I needed to know John was innocent. On the other hand, since I was asking questions up here anyway, I might be able to get in a few about the murder without anybody wondering too much why I was asking. I decided I would ask just enough questions to prove John didn't do it.

I drove the short distance to the Novelli Winery and turned into the parking lot.

"I'm afraid the tour left quite a while ago—" Diane stopped when she recognized me. She was wearing a T-shirt with the winery logo and jeans, and her light brown hair hung loose. She still looked strained.

"I don't think I could take another tour," I said smiling, wanting to put her at ease.

"No, I guess you wouldn't want to." Diane tried to smile.

"This must have been a rough couple of days for you. I almost didn't expect to find you here."

"Well, yes, it has been kind of tough. First the problem here, and then Will—he's the sheriff's deputy, you must have met him, and—"

"I heard," I said, nodding encouragement.

"I really liked Will a lot."

"He seemed like a nice man. Did you know him well?"

"Not really. But the last couple of days, he was around, talking to us, you know, and he was nice."

"Talking to you. About the 'problem' in the wine cellar?"

"Yeah. Will asked me questions and everything, but I couldn't tell him anything. Sometimes I don't go in there for days."

"Don't you go in to get wines for the tasting room?"

"No. Francesca sets that up. But as you can see, we have cases of the wines out here. We would only go into the cellars if someone wanted a bottle or a case of something special."

"Does that mean Francesca wouldn't go into the cellars either?"

90

"She goes in with the tours—and the family might want a bottle of one of the Special Reserve wines with dinner or for guests or something. When her father is here, they drink more of the good wines."

"Has he been here a lot lately?"

"Yeah, more than usual, I think. Most of the time, he comes and goes a lot."

More than usual. That wouldn't mean anything. With the "problem," he would naturally be around more than usual.

"What about Eva?"

"She's almost never here—except she stopped by a few days ago, with Johnny, to have lunch with her grandfather."

"What day?"

"I'm not sure."

"Before or after the body was found?"

That was too blunt. Diane couldn't handle that one. Before she could come up with a reply, Francesca walked into the room, still addressing the tour over her shoulder. Business as usual.

". . . and if you like the wine, we invite you to buy a bottle for the picnic area and a case to take home," she finished. She turned and saw me, then turned back to her little group, shepherding them to the counter and answering their questions about wine. I waited until she was finished.

"My father isn't here today," Francesca said coolly.

"I didn't expect him to be—" I stopped, sensing that was the wrong thing to say. "I came to see you. I just wanted you to know how impressed I am by your self-possession, by the capable way you handled everything the other day."

Francesca relented a little. "Thank you. That was nice of you."

"And I just wondered if you had remembered anything about the night before, anything that might have had to do with the murder."

"Why do you want to know?"

Because I wanted to hear something that would prove John

innocent. And I didn't know how I could explain that to Francesca.

"Well, I was here, and there was so little in the paper," I trailed off lamely. I was going to have to work on my excuse.

"It doesn't matter," Francesca saved me with a little smile. "There's nothing I can tell you anyway. And I have to go back to work now."

"Well, thank you," I said, holding out my hand.

"You're welcome," Francesca said, taking the hand briefly, before dropping it and walking away.

Diane was busy at the tasting bar, and there didn't seem much point in waiting. I trudged back to my car.

Once more, I turned toward town, not the highway. I stopped at the gas station phone booth.

This time Eva herself answered the office phone. She agreed to meet me at the ranch in half an hour and gave directions.

The drive to the Circlecross Ranch wound down through the mountains to the north of Santa Barbara. Just like the road to the south, there were golden hills dotted with scrub oak, and then one sudden curve in the road that was followed by a blinding flash of the sun low over a bright blue ocean.

Despite the clarity of Eva's instructions, I would have missed the turnoff to the ranch if it weren't for the sign. I had been right about the brand.

The house looked ramshackle. It had strange angles that bespoke of rooms added at various times in its long life, and it was badly in need of a paint job. A deep porch stretched across the front of the house. As I pulled to a stop, three large dogs came running up to the car, two large reddish retrievers and a collie. They wriggled with anticipation. One of the retrievers had a blue rubber ball in his mouth.

"Hi," I said to them cautiously. Even though they looked friendly, I wanted to make sure. There was a lot of wriggling and panting going on, but no barking. The retriever with the ball hung his front paws over the door of the Alfa and held his mouth out hopefully. I took the ball out of his mouth and tossed it. All three chased pell-mell after it, affording me an opportunity to get out of the car. They were back before I was halfway to the porch. The dog with the ball kept butting against me. This time, I had to wrestle with him a little to get the ball away. But the toss once again sent the three of them scurrying.

Two more tosses got me to the front door. The woman who opened the door was slender, thirtyish, wearing faded jeans and a man's blue work shirt. She had short, dark wash-and-wear hair. Without makeup, she was beautiful, with her father's dark skin and dark brows and clear, intelligent blue eyes.

"They didn't bark," she said.

"No," I replied. "They may be the friendliest dogs I've ever met. Were they supposed to bark?"

"Absolutely. They *always* bark. Particularly Baskerville."

The retriever started butting me again, and I grabbed for the ball. The game had changed a bit, however. The dog jerked his mouth away before I could quite get it, danced around, and then came back and butted me again.

"Give me the ball, damn it," I said.

Eva laughed. "He knows he's found a sucker. He won't let up—he'll be after you to play with him as long as you're here."

I gave the ball a good toss, and Eva opened the door so that I could come inside before the dogs could return.

"Is the one with the ball Baskerville? He couldn't bark because he had a ball in his mouth."

"No, Baskerville is the collie. The retrievers are Bonnie and Clyde."

We walked into one of those living rooms that look as if they've been put together out of the bits and pieces that everyone brought with them from other lives. The room was dominated by a large television set and the tired green sofa that faced it. Two Queen Anne chairs had shiny cream-colored upholstery. There were also some chairs that looked as if they might have once been in an office. The bookshelves were crowded, books overflowing onto the coffee table. A couple of small tables next to the chairs didn't match. The fireplace hadn't been cleaned since the last time it had been used, probably six months before. One large lamp had evidently come with the owner of the Queen Anne chairs. Two smaller ones looked tired enough to have come from the Salvation Army thrift shop.

Two women were sitting on the couch, watching the evening news. One was seriously overweight, with frizzy reddish-brown hair. She was wearing jeans and a top that would have been a tent on anyone else but that fit her comfortably. The other was slight and dark, in jeans and a tank top with nothing underneath. A tastefully small red rose was tattooed on her left shoulder. Neither wore makeup. Eva introduced them as her housemates, Sandy and Terry. Sandy nodded coolly, and Terry glowered, as if I were intruding. Eva explained that another housemate, Carmen, was outside checking livestock and making sure that nothing in the vegetable garden was about to expire from the heat. Her fourth housemate, Debbie, had driven into Buellton to run errands and had taken the three children, Eva's son Johnny and Carmen's two girls, with her.

I was, as always, momentarily distracted by the television. I had given away a faulty set almost two years before, and I had never bothered to replace it. Probably a reaction against all those years in the newsroom, with monitors on constantly. So I was fascinated that people actually sat and watched television, sometimes for hours at a time.

Eva directed me through the living room and into a small den. The furniture here looked like something her father might have thrown out the last time he redecorated—teak desk and chairs and bookcases that matched. The effect had been softened by a number of throw pillows, white with muted orange and rust.

"Now, what can I do for you?" Eva asked.

"As I mentioned on the phone, I'm writing an article about

winemaking. You can talk to me about Santa Clarissa wines, and the Novelli Winery in particular."

Eva frowned.

"I don't know what to say. I'm not really involved there anymore, and why would you want to talk with me?"

"Well, you are one of the Novellis."

"So what?"

"I'm sorry—I realize that this has turned out to be an awkward time—I was at the winery when the body was discovered. And I heard about Will Baca's accident. Maybe I shouldn't have called you."

"Why did you call?"

She looked at me with smooth face, level eyes. I was pinned, I couldn't fly away.

"I need to know your father wasn't involved." I blurted it out.

"Why? What does that have to do with your article on Santa Clarissa wines?"

Fair question. "Could we get back to that?"

She smiled, a bare twitch of a smile. "Okay. You were there when they found Rick?"

"Yes, I was on the tour. I understand you knew him."

Eva shrugged. "Not really. I hadn't seen him in years, I hadn't really known him well, and I didn't like what I knew."

At least I wouldn't have to deal with a grieving friend here.

"Do you know anything more about how he died than what the paper said?"

"Not much. Phil—Phil Grademon, my father's winemaker—called to tell me, and he didn't know much. Parathion, he said, parathion mixed with wine."

"Is parathion easy to get?"

"Yes. We don't use it, but most people with gardens around here probably have some."

"Do you know what Rick was doing in Santa Clarissa?"

"No."

"What was he like? Do you know any reason why someone might want to kill him?"

"He wasn't a nice guy. He hurt people. But that was a long time ago, and I don't know why anyone would want to kill him now," she said in a tone that ended that subject.

There was silence for a moment. We looked at each other. I broke it.

"I'd like to know something about you," I said. "About your life here. You're a therapist?"

"Yes. A feminist therapist."

"That must be difficult, in such a conservative place."

Eva smiled briefly. "It's necessary, in such a conservative place."

"And your—your lifestyle must make it more difficult."

"In some ways, that's true. But I get a lot of referrals—both because of and in spite of my lifestyle. Some women are more comfortable with me because I haven't adopted mainstream values. And there aren't a lot of feminist therapists around, especially outside the big cities, and even in places like Santa Barbara women are wise enough to be wary of male therapists."

"Why do you put it like that? Why 'be wary of'?"

"Let's take a walk. I don't feel like sitting and talking. And maybe I can interest you in writing an article on feminist therapy instead of murder in the wine industry."

"Maybe so."

I was a little amused and more than a little impressed by Eva's passion for her calling.

The dogs were waiting on the front porch, Clyde with his ball.

"Don't get him started again," she cautioned.

I patted his head and walked with Eva around the side of the house and through a gate into a field. The dogs bounded along. A path led along the edge of the field, where we could walk together.

"Women in our society get a mixed cultural message," she began. "As children, we're taught that good girls are sweet, passive, and dependent. But if we're passive and dependent, we can't grow up to be healthy adults. We're taught that to

96

be happy, we have to belong to a man, to derive our sense of self from the attachment to other. But the reality for most women is that we spend much of our lives not attached to men—either through choice or necessity. Does that mean we're condemned to misery?"

I smiled, starting to like her. "If you're seriously asking that question, I'm the wrong person. I broke an engagement at twenty-five—it was rebound after someone left me, and it was all wrong—and I know what you're saying about child-hood messages, because it was harder for me to tell my father that I wasn't going to get married than it was for me to tell the guy."

"Your father, not your mother?"

"My mother was already dead."

"Sorry."

"It doesn't matter now. Anyway, since I broke the engage-ment, I've cultivated a cheerful self-sufficiency. Although it hasn't always been easy. And I'm not saying that there haven't been ties that bound." I thought of Tom, and winced. I hadn't thought of him for a while. I thought of John, and wondered how I should tell Eva I was interested in her father. Sticky.

"I know," she nodded. "It's in relationships with men that it's hardest to maintain one's center, because that's when the old training comes back and hits one in the heart. I've chosen to separate myself from men entirely, but I realize that's not the way for everyone."

"What about Will? And your son?"

Eva shot me a sidewise glance. "How long have you been asking questions? And who told you what?"

"I'm sorry," I answered, embarrassed. "I don't want to open anything painful as far as Will is concerned. But you don't seem to be mourning him. And I've already told you I'm curious."

We passed through the far side of the field and continued walking beside an irrigation ditch.

"I've been putting bits and pieces together from what your

father said, and your grandfather, and a couple of people at other wineries," I continued.

"I'm sure there's still a lot of gossip," she said, apparently without rancor. "This valley is a very spread-out small town. I make a necessary exception for my son. I didn't see much of Will, except to discuss Johnny's welfare. We co-parented politely, but at a distance. My marriage to him was so long ago, and lasted such a short time, that it almost seems as if it happened to someone else. I lost a semester in college while I was pregnant, but then I took Johnny and went back to school. I allowed my father to help me through graduate school, and I'm grateful to him for that, because it would have been very difficult without him, even with fellowships. He paid, even though he didn't approve of what I was doing. But then, I don't approve of what he does, either."

I backed away from that one.

"Why was he so angry with Will?"

"When I told Will I was leaving, he beat me up. Badly. My father never forgave him for that, and he holds Will responsible for my feelings about men and society. Of course, he could never hold himself responsible."

I was surprised. Will had looked like a good ol' boy, but I wouldn't have guessed he was a wife beater. He had seemed too good-natured for that, not the type to have a violent temper.

We walked on up the hill, then turned to confront a view that started with the small house and the vegetable garden, a patch of greens surrounded by the dry gold of the dying grass, swept on across the valley with its gridded squares of green vines and dark earth, and up the other side.

"Do you know of anything that would connect John with Rick Clarence?"

"Nothing at all." Eva fixed me with her level eyes again. "Are you seeing my father? Is that why you're more interested in the family and the murder than in wine?"

"I'm not sure I'm exactly seeing him." I was embarrassed,

telling her that. I was maybe two years older than she was, and it felt funny.

"But you might be. I thought so." She shook her head. "I'm sorry. I like you, and I hope you don't become involved with him. He has his good qualities, and a lot of women find him attractive, but he hurts them. He hurts women who get too close to him."

"Does that include your sister Francesca?"

"Francesca most of all. He has hurt her by encouraging her to stay with him. And she will, you know, she'll never leave him."

"Do you understand why?"

"No. Neither does he."

We walked back in silence. When we reached the gate of the field close to the house, I wrested the ball from Clyde and threw it.

"I couldn't resist," I said.

"It's fairly safe to indulge irresistible impulses with dogs," Eva said dryly. "But watch it with men—especially my father. Be careful."

She held out her hand and I took it. We smiled at each other and both turned away, Eva to the house and I to my car.

"Oh—one more thing," I called. "Do you know who Will might have been planning to talk to at Davis? What professor Rick Clarence might have been close to?"

She shook her head. "Ask Phil. He'd know."

"Thanks."

I drove to the Grademon Winery, but both winery and house appeared deserted. A sign on the door of the tasting room said that it would reopen at ten the next morning. I was feeling too tired and too stressed to even consider going all the way back to L.A. for the night.

The same room was available at the Mission Inn. I'd simply have to ask enough questions about winemaking—not just about John—to justify charging it to expenses. Although the winemaking article seemed far less compelling to me now than it had a week before.

I woke up in the night and reached out for John. I was sorry he wasn't there.

7

By quarter to ten, I was checked out of the inn and on my way up the curving road to the Grademon Winery.

The house, which had recently been painted a shade of pink seldom seen on a house north of the Mexican border, still looked closed and empty, but the door to the tasting room was open. I had hoped to get to Phil without seeing his unpleasant friend, but resigned myself to the inevitable. It was, however, Phil who was behind the table, still setting up glasses and bottles for the day. His bunchy body was covered by an orange and brown sport shirt. It didn't help.

"What would you like to try?" he asked, gesturing toward the blackboard listing the day's offerings.

It hadn't occurred to me that he wouldn't remember me. But then, he had hardly looked at me. And he had been upset. Devastated.

"I don't know where to start," I said.

"What about the 1984 Sauvignon Blanc?"

"No—I mean, fine, sure."

He poured the requisite small amount for me. I took a sip, found it tart, and then was really at a loss for words. With Phil the winemaker at both places, why did the Novelli wines taste better? I decided to skip the song and dance about my article on wine.

"I was talking to Eva Novelli—" I began.

He waited for me to continue, and when I didn't, he said, "Eva's a friend. I've known her a long time. She got me the job with her father, you know."

"Phil, I need your help," I said, hoping bluntness would work. "I think the person who killed Rick Clarence may have arranged Will Baca's accident. And I need any information you can give me that will help me figure out who it was."

Phil's face twisted, and I thought he might start crying again. His eyes were watery and pink-rimmed. I looked straight into them, praying he would control himself, not wanting to have to comfort him, not believing I could. He didn't cry.

"I don't know what to tell you," was all he said.

"May I ask you some questions?"

"Okay."

"I understand you kept in touch with Rick."

"Not exactly. Vincent would tell me sometimes what Rick was doing."

"Vincent?"

"Vincent Perry. A professor at Davis. A good friend."

"Was he the person Will Baca was on his way to see?"

"I think so. When Will asked me about Davis, I told him about Vincent, too."

Good. Now I had a place to start when I went to Davis. That was certainly better than wandering around the Oenology Station hoping I could stumble into someone who remembered Phil and Rick.

"Did you know Rick was coming to Santa Clarissa?"

"Yes. He called."

"Rick did?"

102

"Yes."

I hoped he would keep going, but he didn't.

"For the first time in all these years?"

"Yes. He'd written sometimes, not often, but he hadn't called, ever."

"What did he say?"

"Just that he was coming."

"Did he tell you why he was coming, or who he wanted to see?"

"He said he had business. And he wanted to see me." Phil's voice wavered on the last word.

"He had business with you?"

"No. But he wanted to see me."

"Did you see him?"

This was dangerous ground. Phil's face was starting to twist again. I was keeping my voice as soft as I could, carefully modulated, fighting desperation that wanted to translate into stridency, not wanting to push him but needing to hear his answers.

"No."

"Do you have any idea who did see him?"

"No."

"Is there anyone around here other than you and Eva who knew Rick?"

"I don't know."

"Could he have had business with John?"

"John Novelli? I don't know. Why? Why would he have business with John Novelli?"

How could I answer? What else could I ask? I felt as if I were dealing with a marshmallow. Then Phil changed.

"Hi, Michael," he said softly, a different, warmer person. I saw him smile for the first time. His dimples showed, and he was almost pretty.

I turned. The young man I had met earlier was standing in the doorway, glaring at me.

"Weren't you just leaving?" he snapped.

I met his gaze for a moment, then turned back to Phil.

"Okay. Well, I guess that's everything. Thanks."

He shrugged, went back to setting up glasses. Michael came in and joined him, ignoring me. I left the glass Phil had given me on the counter, still with its bit of tart wine.

Michael is such an asshole, I thought. Why is Phil so enamored?

I got into the Alfa and slammed it into gear. I was still annoyed as I started negotiating the curves that would take me down the other side of the hill to the road leading to Highway 101. That would take me to 680, which connected with Interstate 80, and hence to Davis.

The road was as curvy and mountainous as the one up from Santa Barbara, and just as lonely and beautiful, although August was not its best month. I guessed that the countryside was brown most of the year, however. Maybe it turned green in February. It's a cliché about California, but it's true—green in the winter, brown and gold in the summer.

I was two or three miles from the winery when I realized something was wrong. I was cheerfully breezing down the mountainside, just a little too fast for a road I didn't know, when I heard a kind of grating noise, as if I were dragging something beneath the car. I was puzzled, because I couldn't remember driving over anything. The noise wasn't the engine, whatever it was. Then the car started pulling slightly to the right. Before I could decide what to do about it, I saw a wheel hurtle down the road ahead of me, and a sudden twist in my stomach, the lurch of terror when the bottom has just fallen out of the elevator, told me the wheel had belonged to the Alfa.

I didn't hit the brakes. I'm not sure why, except that the original wearer of the Ferrari jacket had drummed that into my head years before, and it stuck. In an emergency, don't hit the brakes unless you're sure it's the right thing to do. I wasn't. So I hit the accelerator instead, turning the steering wheel slightly toward the left, heading for the shoulder. Don't fall over till I get there, I begged. And please, dear God, don't let anybody come around that corner until I'm off the road! I steered for a thick clump of dried-out wildflowers and turned off the ignition as I finally stepped on the brake pedal. The car clunked onto the right side of the front axle, where the wheel had been, bounced, and stopped. I fell forward, clutching the wheel, head against my hands.

When I looked up, I saw that just beyond the clump of wildflowers there was a steep drop down the side of the mountain. I started to shake, shivering even as the sun fried my shoulders. I put my head back down against my hands.

Something inside me wouldn't quite function. I couldn't let go of the steering wheel, couldn't leave the car. I knew I had to get help, knew I couldn't stay on the highway, but I didn't know how I would ever be able to move. I concentrated on my fingers, just trying to make my fingers work.

I heard a car engine next to me.

"Need help?"

"I think so," I said in a small voice.

The car pulled over and stopped and the door slammed. Footsteps crunched toward me.

"Jesus! You ought to be dead!"

"Thanks for the vote of confidence."

"Mom! Is that you?"

That jolted me. I looked up into the smiling face of Russ Cahill.

"Hi," I said weakly. "Yeah. It's me. And it's no picnic."

He chuckled, patting me on the back. "You're some driver, Mom. You should be over that cliff right now, spun out and overturned. Come on. Let's look for your wheel and call a tow truck."

I took my cap off and stuck it in my purse, shaking my hair out. I looked to make sure that I had locked everything in the trunk and took the hand he held out to me.

"Thanks, kid," I said, my voice a little stronger.

He drove slowly, periodically pulling over so that we could look down gullies. We found the wheel about half a mile down the road and a couple of hundred feet over the side. He bounded down and clambered back up with the wheel, tossing it into the back seat of the yellow Mercedes 450SL.

"Your other mother is going to love that," I commented.

"You think she'd want me to leave you stranded?"

"She might."

Russ grinned. "You'd really like her if you knew her. You two just have a communication problem."

I didn't think that was true. What I said was, "You may be right. Where do we go now?"

"Polarity is closest. Do you have an Auto Club card?"

"I do, but this is still going to cost me. There can't be any place within five miles. Where should I have it towed?"

"Back to Los Robles. That's where the tow truck will be from anyway. You wouldn't want them to mess with your engine, but I think they can do okay with the body work, and that's all it needs. How'd you manage to lose a wheel?"

"I haven't the vaguest idea."

He turned onto a dirt road that I hadn't even noticed. That we bounced only a little was due to the magic of German shock absorbers. The dirt road became a driveway with a cluster of sheds at the end. Russ pulled up in front of one of them, hopped out, and yelled, "Cindy?"

The woman who appeared from one of the farther sheds looked like a Rapunzel who had just let down her long, pale gold hair, if you could imagine a wide-eyed, smiling Rapunzel in a denim skirt and flowery cotton blouse. How could someone named Cindy Frawn look so much like a fairy-tale princess, I mused. Maybe this Cinderella's prince just happened to be a drop-out turned winemaker. Cindy Frawn's hair floated around her like a perfect take for a television commercial.

Bounding along beside her was a beautiful black and silver dog that looked almost like a German shepherd, but the coat was wrong. As the dog trotted up to sniff, I saw that she had one blue eye and one brown eye, the first time I had ever seen a dog with eyes like that. I held out my hand for the dog to sniff. The dog not only sniffed but nuzzled, wanting to be petted. I obliged.

Russ introduced me to Cindy.

"Hi," she said. "What can I help you with?"

"I had a problem with my car, and I need to call the Auto Club. Do you mind if I use your phone? It must be a toll call—I'll pay you for it."

Cindy wouldn't hear of my paying to call a tow truck. She led us toward the shed that served as a house, the dog dancing along.

"Tell me about your dog," I said. "What kind is she? What's her name? She's amazingly beautiful."

"She's half German shepherd and half Siberian husky, her name is Tessa, and she knows she's beautiful."

Inside, the shed looked a lot better than it did from outside. More than that—it had a good feeling in it. One corner was partitioned off—I hoped it was a bathroom, and it was—but the rest of it was one large, airy room, with cooking space, eating space, sitting space, and sleeping space. The furniture was mostly hand-hewn wood and hand-sewn pillows, as if everything had been done from scratch. There was a lot of color, white daisies and blue lupine and orange poppies, as if summer had hit the room. Glass jars full of wildflowers were on every available surface.

I called the tow truck and gratefully accepted Cindy's offer of herb tea when I discovered the truck would be at least an hour. There was only one in the area, and it was out on another call. They would telephone me when it was on its way. I asked Russ if this was a problem for him, but he was apparently enjoying the rescue, and said he'd hang around until I got safely back to Los Robles with the car.

Cindy wanted to know what happened, and I told her only the immediate part of it, plus my original reason for being in the valley.

"I had planned on getting in touch with you," I added. "I thought you'd be a good person to interview for the article. This obviously isn't a good time for me—I think I'm still

107

shaking too much to remember anything you tell me. But I'd like to come and talk with you again."

Cindy appeared delighted at the prospect. I found her presence calming. I leaned back into the cushions, Tessa lying across my feet. I wanted to sit and drink herb tea all afternoon, talk about cats and dogs and gardens, exchange recipes. I wanted to ask if living with Prince Charming—if indeed Cinderella had found him—was all it was cracked up to be.

I was sorry when the phone rang, when I had to leave. Going back to the real world meant coping with a damaged Alfa miles from the nearest authorized dealer. And I didn't want to think about that. I promised to call Cindy soon, to see her again.

We got back to the car about ten minutes ahead of the tow truck. The driver was young, maybe a couple of years older than Russ. He looked like a cousin of the Santa Clarissa gas station attendant. And he didn't think he should tow the car—or at least not on my Auto Club card.

"This here isn't mechanical trouble. This here's an accident. I'm not supposed to tow accidents," he told me.

"Please tow it back to your garage," I said, calmly seething. "If the owner has any problem accepting my Auto Club card, I'll certainly pay whatever he thinks fair."

Finally, Russ had to intercede. Grudgingly, the driver agreed to tow the car, but only because a local vouched for me. He nevertheless made me sign a release saying I wouldn't hold him responsible if the bumper were damaged by the tow.

At the moment, a soft bumper was the least of my problems and I signed, dreaming of hoisting him on his own tow hook.

I rode with Russ, following the tow truck back. Russ waited while I discovered that the wheel was bent and the axle was damaged, that they couldn't tell me immediately why the wheel flew off, and that I would either have to have the Alfa towed to Santa Barbara or leave it until they could get the parts—at least three days, maybe longer if they had to get them from Los Angeles. And there weren't any rental cars available, not in Los Robles.

108

"How about a horse?" I asked.

Only Russ found it funny.

I left the car.

"Where to now?" he asked, as he helped move my bags from the Alfa to the Mercedes.

"Oh, God, I don't know. The Mission Inn. I need to think."

He drove to the Mission Inn, waited while I checked back in, an act that didn't even elicit a raised eyebrow from the smiling woman who had checked me out only hours before, and carried my bags up to the same room.

"Thanks," I said.

"No problem," he said. He started out, then stopped. "Hey—did you mean it about a horse?"

"Sort of. Why?"

"Just that if you want to ride, I could take you to a ranch tomorrow."

I thought about my options for the next day. There weren't many.

"I'd really like that. Thanks."

"See you tomorrow, Mom," he said and left, grinning as always.

What now, I thought. I walked down to the lobby and telephoned the sheriff's office in Santa Clarissa. I reached a recording that informed me no one was available to answer the phone at the moment and offered me another number to call in case of emergency. This didn't seem to be an emergency—probably a good thing in this area—so I didn't call the other number. In any case, I wasn't sure how I could explain over the phone my ugly growing awareness that I had almost been killed in the same kind of accident that Will Baca had fallen victim to.

On an impulse, I dialed John Novelli's private line in Santa Clarissa. I reached a recording there, too, this one offering his Los Angeles number. I left a message, saying only that my plans had changed because of car trouble and I would be at the Mission Inn for the next few days. On another impulse, I called the Circlecross Ranch.

Eva was there. I told the same story to Eva, and asked if she wanted to drive to Santa Clarissa for dinner. She did. We agreed on seven-thirty.

I waited for Eva in the small cocktail lounge. A cool shower had restored my body, and a cool glass of Chardonnay was restoring my soul. I had been certain that Eva would not dress up for the occasion, so I had chosen a fringed denim skirt and blouse. I had been right. She was wearing natural cotton pants and vest with a white tailored shirt.

The headwaiter greeted Eva by name and seated us at a table with a view of a spacious patio. Eva barely glanced at the menu, then ordered sea bass grilled, no sauce, and the house salad. I ordered the same. I was still shaky from the afternoon, and didn't want to make a decision about food. Eva chose the wine.

"Thank you for coming," I said once the waiter had left. "I really needed company tonight."

Eva nodded. "Tell me what happened."

"I had car trouble—I lost a wheel. This afternoon. The same accident that Will Baca had. Why would somebody want to kill me?"

"What makes you think somebody wants to kill you?"

"Do you really think Will's death was an accident?"

"Of course."

"And you think it's a coincidence that I almost had the same accident?"

"I think that's the most likely explanation. What's yours?"

"Mine is that I think Will was murdered—by the same person who killed Rick Clarence. Because Will was on the right track, would have made an arrest. And because I told the deputy I didn't think it was an accident, because I was going to Davis to talk with Vincent Perry, the same person Will wanted to see, trying to find out what happened, the person who murdered Rick Clarence and Will Baca tried to kill me."

"I suppose that's possible."

"But you don't believe it."

110

Eva shrugged a therapist shrug, implying that it wasn't important whether or not she believed it.

"You're right," I said, laughing nervously. "If someone told me a story like that, my reaction would be to start singing the Paranoia Chorus."

"Paranoia is hardly a word I'd use. What happened this afternoon obviously frightened you a lot. Do you want to talk about it?"

I did want to talk about it.

When I finished, Eva said, "Russ was right—you're lucky. But you wouldn't have thought it was anything other than an accident if Will hadn't lost a wheel."

"No, of course not," I admitted.

"Why not?"

"Well, because I can't imagine anyone wanting to kill me. And because only a few people knew I had stopped by the sheriff's office, or that I planned on going to Davis, and I don't like suspecting any of them."

"Who were they?"

I hesitated. "Alida Cahill knew I was going to talk with Jerry Harris. Phil Grademon knew I was going to Davis. Your father knew both."

Eva's mouth twitched. "Are you asking me to consider seriously that Alida Cahill, Phil Grademon, or my father murdered Rick, murdered Will, and tried to murder you?"

"I guess not. I guess it does sound pretty unlikely, doesn't it?" I wasn't sure that it was all that unlikely. But I had no arguments at hand to convince Eva, particularly since John seemed the most likely culprit. How could Alida have gimmicked the wheel? Or Phil, given the short time between our conversation and my mishap?

"How about preposterous? If you're seeing my father—I think under the circumstances you might let me know just what is going on there."

"We went to the theater and a wine tasting in Los Angeles over the weekend, and we may have started something. I wouldn't call it anything serious, though." The word "yet" hung unspoken.

"You might not. But Alida might—it's enough to make Alida jealous, although hardly murderous. And my father's reputation as a lady-killer is not meant to be taken literally. I'm sure the passion you aroused in him was of quite another kind." She reached over and patted my hand, letting me know it was okay. "Besides, leaving Will aside for the moment, I don't think either Alida or my father knew Rick. And I just can't believe Phil would have murdered him, especially not after all these years. So what happens to your theory?"

"Preposterous is the word for it."

The waiter brought our salads.

"Right," Eva continued when the waiter had left. "Look, I know Rick was poisoned by a person or persons unknown in my family's wine cellar. I don't like thinking that it was someone I know, maybe someone I've known for a long time. For one thing, this valley has been home to me full-time for the last four years, and part-time a lot longer than that, and I really care about some of these people. For another, I like to think I have some insight into people, into who they are and why they do what they do. And I can't think of anyone around here who would commit murder. And you're asking me to imagine that someone I know, someone who is close to me, is committing multiple murders, which just becomes—" Eva shrugged again.

"Preposterous."

"Right."

"But Rick's murderer had to be someone you know, didn't it? How else could the body have gotten into your father's wine cellar?"

"I don't know. But Phil didn't do it, and my father didn't do it, and Francesca didn't do it, and they're the only people who had keys."

"You don't have a key?"

"I have a key to the house, but not to the wine cellar."

"What about access to a key?"

112

"That's a little more complicated. My father has always kept spare keys to everything—house, cars, winery—on hooks inside a kitchen cabinet. So anyone who had access to the house had access to the keys."

"Do you know who had access to the house?"

Eva shook her head. "In theory, anyone who knows any member of the family. Strangers were never particularly welcome, but friends—anybody's friends—always were."

"And anybody could have known about the keys?"

"Right. Anybody who was a friend."

We sat in silence for a moment.

"I'm sorry, I really am," I told her.

Eva smiled faintly. "It's not your fault."

I didn't want to leave the subject, but I did want to ease the air a little. "How long was it since you had seen Rick Clarence?" I asked.

The waiter arrived with our entrees. Eva had barely touched her salad, but gave it away to the waiter anyway. I had finished mine, sopping up the dressing with a piece of bread. The dissipation of the afternoon's terror had left me hungry.

"I hadn't seen him or heard from him since I left Davis."

"Did anyone besides you and Phil know Rick? Will told me there were a couple of people—did he just mean the two of you?"

"I don't know of anyone else."

"Would Phil know?"

"He might, he might not."

I was going to have to ask him—if I could get past the surge of terror I felt at the prospect of driving out there again.

"How would you feel about telling me what kind of relationship the three of you had at Davis? I'm confused about the time frame, by the way—were you there before your father bought the winery?"

Eva finished the bite of fish that was in her mouth and took a sip of wine before she replied.

"There's no reason not to tell you the story if you want to

113

hear it, but I don't think it has anything to do with Rick's murder."

Eva paused, and I waited for her to continue.

"We all knew—Mama, Francesca, and I—that my father dreamed of his own winery. Years before he bought the land, we would come up here sometimes, just drive up for lunch on a Saturday, to look at the country. Francesca and I fell in love with it, too, although Mama never did. So my decision to go to Davis was based more on my love of the central valleys than anything else, I think. And I wanted to learn something about wine—I took a couple of courses in oenology, with the idea that I might become his winemaker. My father wanted that too, a lot. But I discovered that it wasn't something I wanted to do. Phil was a teaching assistant; he taught the lab for the first class I took, and we became buddies. He had a real flair—it was obvious even then—and I really admired his skill. He was shy, and he liked it that someone admired him. I don't really think Rick did."

"He and Rick were lovers?"

"Yes, although I don't think many people were aware of it. They were very discreet, and I think most people assumed they were simply roommates. After I met Will, I didn't see as much of them. I was starry eyed, and Will was not the type to pal around with a couple of gay guys, no matter how discreet they were."

Eva said "starry eyed" so dryly, so matter-of-factly, that it was hard to imagine. She appeared to be a woman who had never lost her head over a man and never would. I had to work to see her at eighteen, a different woman.

"Will was a year ahead of me. I took a course in political science while I was floundering around looking for a major, and that was how I met him—that was his major. He always planned on coming back here to be a cop. His highest ambition was to run for county sheriff, and I think he would have made it. We wanted to get married, and my parents didn't approve, so I got pregnant. They still didn't approve, but they decided to acquiesce. They were right, of course." Eva

114

smiled, remembering who she was at the time, forgiving her. Then she went on. "This seems foolish to me now, but Will and I hadn't talked about what we were going to do when he graduated. I assumed that I would somehow commute to classes. He assumed I would quit school. I grew up in a hurry. And I left him. He saw that as an attack somehow—and I guess some of the things I said were pretty brutal—and he had to fight back. He ran out of words. I understand that now, although I didn't at the time. Actually, I didn't get into psychology until I got back to school, after we broke up."

"And you started seeing Phil and Rick again?"

"Seeing Phil. Rick had left him. I couldn't have made it through those months, going to school and taking care of Johnny, if it hadn't been for Phil. And I don't think he could have made it if it hadn't been for us. He was really heartbroken over Rick. And it was okay for Johnny, too. He's a straight-A student, and I know it's because of those early years, when Phil and I were both there studying all the time."

"How did you ever come to terms with Will, to let him see so much of Johnny?"

"My grandfather intervened. You met him, didn't you?"

"Yes. And he's irresistible—even more so than your father."

"Exactly. Will had the sense to go to him, and Tony asked me to work something out with Will about Johnny. I couldn't refuse him. I think my father wouldn't like my saying this, but there are ways in which Tony is still the head of the family. Besides, in retrospect, I know he was right. Will had a right to share his son, although I had trouble seeing that. Will was the best father he knew how to be."

That was the best compliment she knew how to give.

I pushed my plate away.

"Look, I know I'm eating faster than you are. Do you mind if I order coffee?"

"No. I'm not really that hungry anyway. Coffee is a good idea."

We agreed on decaffeinated cappuccino, and flagged the waiter down.

"This doesn't have anything to do with what we were talking about," I said when the cappuccino arrived, in regular cups, with the steamed milk and a sprinkle of cinnamon on top, "but what is your mother like?"

"Why do you want to know?"

"That's not fair. You know why I want to know."

Eva looked me straight in the eyes. "Watch out. He's dangerous."

"A killer?"

"No, not that. At least, I don't think so. But I've told you. He hurts women."

"Yes, you have. And I appreciate that. I'll be as careful as I can, although I'm not sure how careful that is. He's very seductive."

"Yes, I know."

Eva's words sat there, kind of ugly, and I didn't want to ask what she meant. I chose my words before I continued.

"Is your mother okay?"

"She's fine. She's never really recovered the piece of her identity she lost, living all those years with him, but she has her hair done once a week, and her nails done once a week, and she has the house in Bel Air, and she does a lot of volunteer work for Catholic charities, and people love her, they think she's very special. And I think she's more or less happy."

"That's about as okay as anybody ever is."

"Yes."

"And while we're on the subject, why would Alida Cahill be jealous of me?"

Eva rolled her eyes. "Come on. You know why. Only God, Alida, and my father know what happened, and Alida and my father have different versions of it. I think she probably made more of it than it was—and then she started denying anything ever happened—but I also think he honestly doesn't realize how much he promises with his eyes, his voice, his sweat, his cock, whatever."

"I think you're right. Why does Alida go out of her way to deny it, though?"

"There's a lot of self-deception in Alida's life, and I think there has been ever since her husband left her for another woman. She drinks a lot, as you may have noticed, and it's not unusual for heavy drinkers to develop patterns of denial. She wants everyone to believe that she runs the winery herself, but she never would have made it without Henri Cheverin. I wish, for her sake, that she were really as capable as she claims to be. And I think she might be, if she stopped drinking and took charge."

"Henri Cheverin—the original winemaker at Novelli?"

"Yes."

"What happened that caused him to leave?"

Eva shrugged. "Nothing. Or I don't know, I guess. I really haven't followed the affairs of the winery as closely as I might have."

"How do I get in touch with him?"

"He's at the Lindale Winery now."

I made a mental note to drop by the Lindale Winery. I had to do that anyway, sooner or later. We finished our cappuccinos, and I picked up the check.

"We're eating on *Explore!*," I told her.

As we got up to leave, I held out my arms. "Good night. And thank you."

Eva walked into them and hugged me back. "Good night."

Eva left, and I went to my room. I had picked up a paperback mystery, and I read well into the night, wishing I hadn't given up Valium, and, when exhaustion outweighed terror, I fell asleep.

I was awakened by a pounding at the door.

"Just a minute," I shouted, disoriented, fumbling for my robe, wondering where I was. "Who is it?"

I couldn't understand the mumble filtered through the heavy oak door. I found my robe on the floor, where it had evidently fallen when I kicked it off the bed sometime in the night.

The sliver of light spilling through the crack where the heavy, flowered drapes came together was my only cue that it was morning. I had forgotten to set my travel clock. I was, however, certain that it was too early for anyone to have a good reason to pound on my door.

"Who is it?" I shouted again, once my robe was on and I was next to the door.

"It's me—Russ—remember? Let's go," was the shouted reply.

I opened the door, eyes still blurry, my head unfocused as well.

"This is a joke, right? What time is it?"

"It's a little after nine," he said, grinning brightly. He was wearing jeans and boots and an old cowboy hat, and through my fogged eyes he looked like the Sundance Kid.

I took a deep breath. "You're too young to see anyone my age at this hour of the morning."

"Come on, Mom, you look great."

I wanted to spit at him. Instead I said calmly, "Come back in fifteen minutes with orange juice and coffee—with cream!"

"Okay," he said, and jogged down the hall.

The first thing I did when he left was open the curtains. The sunlight immediately made me feel better. I had an inside room, overlooking an atrium, and the peaceful view helped, too.

Then I walked into the small bathroom and looked at myself in the mirror.

"Hello, gorgeous," I sighed.

By the time Russ returned bearing a tray with two glasses of orange juice and one mug of coffee, I had washed and dressed. I had brought a pair of jeans, and an old pair of sneakers would just have to do, since I hadn't brought boots.

"Thanks, kid," I said as I sipped the orange juice. "I needed that."

"No problem," he said, beaming at me.

I poured two tiny containers of cream into the mug of coffee. "I'll be right back. I need just a little makeup before I face the day."

"You look great the way you are."

"You lie, but that's fine. Keep lying."

Another fifteen minutes, a little makeup, my hair fluffed out, and I decided I could in fact face the day.

"Okay," I said. *"Now* let's go!"

Walking out into the morning, I marveled at the clarity of the light. Outlines were so sharp, shadows so distinct, colors so bright that even muted shades seemed saturated. The blazing pastels of the buildings made me want to blink. The bougainvillea splashed down the side of the two-story inn like a purple waterfall. The sky was a blue that I had almost forgotten, although I saw it maybe once or twice a year in Los Angeles, the day after a storm. I put my dark glasses on. It was too early for that much truth.

The ranch was on the other side of Santa Clarissa, about five miles past the Novelli Winery. Russ drove through the front gate, parked the Mercedes in front of the gray frame house, and headed for the barn. I didn't see a sign of people.

"Are you sure this is okay?" I asked.

"Oh, yeah, I ride all the time. It's good for the horses to get exercise. I called Andy last night—Andy James, it's his ranch—and told him I'd have a friend with me this morning, and he said fine."

The yard smelled like a combination of dust, hay, and horseshit. The huge barn smelled the same, but worse. There were stalls down both sides, some of them inhabited by shuffling horses. Russ looked at the selection.

"How long since you've ridden?" he asked.

"You don't want to know—or at least I don't want to count."

"You should be okay on Jenny," he said, as he slipped a bridle over the head of a brindled filly and led her out of her stall. He quickly saddled her and helped me mount, then adjusted the stirrups. "Just wait for me in the yard."

Fortunately, Jenny seemed to understand, because she walked easily out of the barn and stopped, gently snorting. I patted her neck, hoping I could remember how to do this. I did remember what I had liked about riding, as a girl—the feeling of freedom, of space, and I realized that this was why I had always had a sports car, because it was as close as I could get to that same feeling in a car. That was what I had liked about Tom's bike. Forget that.

Russ appeared a moment later on a sorrel gelding.

"You sure do sit tall in the saddle, Mom," he said. "I'll bet you wanted to be a cowgirl when you grew up."

120

"No, I wanted to be a cow*boy*. When I was growing up, cowboys got to do all the fun stuff, and cowgirls had to wait back at the ranch. I wanted to be out there with the action. I was certain Dale would understand when Roy left her for me."

"Who?"

"Roy Rogers? Dale Evans?"

"Oh, yeah, I think I've heard of them. Didn't they do a religious show or something?"

"Yeah, kid, something like that."

He led me alongside a field where a dozen horses were grazing and up a dry trail through brush so brown it had to be a fire hazard into the hills behind the ranch. I knew my sinuses were going to clog and hoped I had enough tissues in my pocket to make it through the morning.

"I thought your mother told me that the winemakers and the ranchers weren't particularly friendly," I said, when he dropped back next to me. "How is it that you can saddle up and ride away?"

He didn't answer right away, and when he did, it was without his customary grin.

"Will Baca—do you know about Will?"

I nodded, and he continued.

"Will lived on the ranch here, rented a room, and he was my buddy, particularly after my dad moved out. Will and Johnny and I—Johnny's Will's son—used to go camping together on weekends."

"I'm sorry—it must have been tough for you, what happened to Will."

"Yeah, it was. And it was so strange yesterday, finding you like that, missing a wheel, so close to what happened to him. Wondering if I'd been there, if I could have made a difference for him."

"What difference?"

"I don't know."

"Have you talked to anybody about it?"

"No."

121

"What was Will like?"

"He was really a great guy. I really miss him. You know, Johnny liked to bring his dogs, Bonnie and Clyde, along when we went camping. And Clyde hated the water. Bonnie didn't care—she'd plunge right into a river and splash around. But Clyde would just sit there on the bank, and when we all crossed and pretended we were going on without him, he'd howl like a little kid. So Will would go back and carry him across. Can you imagine that? He'd carry that damn dog across the river, getting himself all wet to do it. Because Johnny wanted to take the dogs. That's what he was like."

We rode on for a while in silence.

"Russ? I think it's wonderful that you loved him. But you couldn't have saved him, you have to know that."

"Yeah, I guess so."

"Listen, I want to report my accident. I don't think telling Jerry will do much good, but he seemed to think someone would be coming up from Santa Barbara, and I want it on record that I was almost taken out by the same kind of accident that got Will. The thing is, I don't think they were accidents, either one. I think someone sabotaged the cars. Do you want to come with me? We can see what else is being done."

"What are you saying? You think somebody killed Will? And tried to kill you?"

"Well, I'm still not sure. I just have trouble believing it's a coincidence, that Will dies when he was investigating a murder, and then that what went wrong with Will's car and what went wrong with mine were the same thing."

"Who would want to kill either you or Will?"

"The person Will was going to arrest for Rick Clarence's murder, whoever that was."

"If you don't know who it was, why would they want to kill you?"

"I don't know that either. And it wouldn't make sense to me anyway. Murder doesn't make sense to me, it really doesn't."

122

"Me neither. And yeah, I would like to go with you to Jerry's office."

"Then let's ride down and do that."

Russ turned off the trail, at an angle, taking us down an easy slope. We were coming out behind Novelli Winery.

"Do you mind if we stop for a minute, to see Tony?" I asked.

"No, that'd be fine."

We passed the barbecue and caught the trail that John and I had walked. As we rode up to the house, I pulled around to the side. Tony was sitting in the same place, on the patio, unchanged since my last visit, even to the unmatched socks.

I tried to slip gracefully from the horse and discovered that my knees had somehow ceased to exist. I had to hold on to Jenny, clinging to the saddle until I recovered a sense of my own legs under me.

"Howdy, pardner," I called to Tony.

He had been watching us ride up.

"Hi," he whispered, nodding.

Russ dismounted easily and tossed his reins around the railing of the patio steps.

"Hi, Tony," he said.

"Hi," Tony whispered, still nodding.

I clumsily wrapped Jenny's reins around the railing and carefully climbed the steps, holding on.

"How are you?" I asked, leaning over to kiss him on his papery forehead.

"Fine," he said, smiling with his whole face, with his soft blue eyes, reaching up with his good hand to take mine. "Good to see you again."

"Good to see you, too. I could use a Perrier with lime, couldn't you, Russ?"

"Yeah, sure."

Tony rang the large old school bell, and Lucy appeared in her starched white uniform.

"Three Perriers with lime," he whispered with authority, gleefully.

"Coming right up, Tony," Lucy said. She smiled briefly at us before she left.

We sat down at the glass-topped table.

Tony looked expectant. Russ looked at the hills. I didn't know what to say.

"Have you seen John?" Tony asked me.

"Yes, I saw him in Los Angeles."

"Good," Tony nodded.

"But I came today to see you."

"Good," Tony nodded again with that little-kid joy.

"Tony, I want you to know how sorry I am about what happened to Will."

Tony's face fell, went slack, and then it re-formed into something strong, something I hadn't seen in him before.

"Thank you," he said, in close to a normal voice. "I appreciate that."

Lucy appeared with our drinks. Tony's face went vacant again, and he motioned us to be silent.

"Thank you," I said to Lucy as she served us.

"You're welcome," Lucy said brightly, but with that same surprise, as if it had been a while since anyone had said those words.

When she left, I said, "How long had it been since you'd seen him?"

"What?" Tony asked, startled.

"Will Baca. How long had it been since you'd seen him?"

"Oh." Tony shrugged. "I don't know. He stopped by."

"When?"

"Not long ago. I liked Will, you know."

"I know."

"Good fellow. Did you know he was married to Eva?"

"Yes, I heard that."

"She shouldn't have left him."

"Tony, did Will have anything special to say when he stopped by?"

Tony stared off at the hills, with Russ. I thought he had forgotten the question, but he finally answered.

124

"No."

I sipped my Perrier in silence. Russ had already finished his. Jenny shuffled and snorted, and the sorrel gelding echoed her.

"Well," I said cheerily, "I guess we ought to be getting the horses back. Next time I come I'm going to bring you some new socks."

Tony looked down at his feet, at the one pale blue sock and the one dark blue sock. His eyes gleamed again.

"Like this one," he said, pointing to the light blue sock. "It's my favorite pair. I only wear one at a time, so they'll last."

I looked carefully at the sock, clearly a softer cotton than its mismate.

"Like that one," I said. "So long, Tony."

"So long."

"See ya, Tony," Russ said, tossing Jenny's reins to me and bounding gracefully onto the sorrel.

"Bye."

I made it up by myself, thighs screaming as they circled the filly again. We headed for the road.

We rode the rest of the way to the sheriff's office in silence. Jerry Harris was there. His car was parked in front and the door was open. This time, I found swinging my leg across Jenny's back even more painful. Whatever had possessed me to think we could do this on horseback? Why weren't we riding blissfully in the Mercedes? Russ dismounted lightly, oblivious to my discomfort.

"Probably it's all a coincidence," Jerry said lamely, after I had told him my story. "And I told you, somebody's going to come up from Santa Barbara in a day or two, and maybe he'll be able to figure it all out, and if it has any connection to the guy in the wine cellar."

"Hey, Jerry, why don't *you* try to figure it out? Didn't Will teach you anything?" Russ had been silent until then.

"Come on, Russ, I didn't figure on no murders when I took this job, you know that. Petty theft, a little vandalism, that kind of shit, you know? Not some guy coming in here and getting murdered, and then Will buying it like that."

"Yeah, I know."

Russ and I looked at each other.

"You ready, kid?"

"Yeah, let's go, Mom."

I had almost forgotten until I got up and straightened my legs that I was going to have to get back on the horse. I considered asking Russ to lead Jenny back to the ranch and pick me up in the car, but I decided that would be like letting the team down, admitting defeat. I took a deep breath and remounted. Russ had already started back to the highway, and I had to trot to catch up with him. First the self-defense workshop, now this. As soon as I got back to Los Angeles, I was going to start a regular exercise program. Maybe I would even get a television set and a VCR, so that I could work out with a cassette. Jane Fonda. If Jane Fonda, almost twenty years older than I, could do it, I could. But Jane Fonda was so compulsive about exercise. I could never be that compulsive about anything.

I wanted to cheer when we rounded a curve and the ranch appeared, even though it was still a half mile away. Jenny picked up the pace, and I didn't try to stop her. I empathized with the horse.

We pulled up next to the barn, and when I slid off the horse I had to hold on again, waiting for my knees to signal that they were willing to function. This time, Russ noticed.

"Got to you, huh, Mom?" he asked, his grin back in place.

"Kid, I confess. Do you mind if I wait for you in the car?"

"Nah, go ahead."

I picked my way carefully to the car, got in and arranged myself, my legs stretching as straight as they could. The pain would go away, I reminded myself, and so would the smell of the horse that had followed me. I hoped it wouldn't forever linger in the Mercedes. It wouldn't, of course—Russ said he rode often. An advantage of convertibles. They aired out.

What physical pain did for one, I thought as I relaxed in the sun, was it made one take not quite so seriously the very real shit that was coming down in one's life. If I had been at home, with all that had happened, I'd be running my finger around the inside of the empty Valium bottle, hoping the dust would help. Instead, I was sitting there contemplating my aching thighs, almost calmly hoping that I could somehow cope with a person or persons unknown who might be trying to kill me. Almost calmly. My stomach knotted, and I wished that I indeed had the Valium bottle.

Russ finally returned, intensifying the smell of horse in the car.

"I need to ask a real favor, kid," I told him.

"Anything, Mom," he answered, and I knew he meant it.

"Be careful what you're thinking. Incest is taboo in these parts, you know."

He laughed.

"I need you to drive me to Santa Barbara so I can rent a car," I continued. "I can't be stuck here for God knows how long with no car. And a horse is just not the same. I tried—God knows I tried—and it didn't work. And neither will my legs, for some time to come, so walking is out of the question."

"You got it." His smile faded. "But first we're going to stop by the garage. I need to know why you lost a wheel."

I was just as glad he was with me when the mechanic told us.

"Bearings froze," he said. "No fluid. Happens sometimes in older cars. Couldn't figure why it would happen to this one—five years old, you say?"

"Yeah. Only five years old. And serviced regularly."

"Can't understand it."

"Neither can I."

Russ drove me to a rent-a-car lot in Santa Barbara. Neither of us had much to say, and I was glad the day was so beautiful that I had scenery to look at, glad my thighs were sore so I had something besides murder to think about.

He waited while I arranged for a red Ford Escort. I liked the sound of it better than the appearance. I was trying to learn how to limp on both feet, not putting any weight on either leg, when I returned to the Mercedes.

"Thanks, kid."

"Keep in touch, Mom."

"I will."

We grinned at each other. I started to limp away.

"Hey, Mom? Maybe I'll stop by tomorrow morning, make sure you're okay?"

"Okay, kid."

He drove away, pausing to wave as he left the lot.

My grand plans for the afternoon—going back to talk with Cindy Frawn, and then up to the Lindale Winery to see Henri Cheverin—were short-circuited by a need to soak my aching muscles in a tub. And there was a message at the desk. John had called. I thought about that while I soaked.

Did I believe that John had tried to kill me? I didn't want to believe that. But did I believe that John was capable of killing someone, some abstract person, who got in his way, who somehow threatened what he wanted? Yes. I did. And I was still attracted to him, and I didn't know what to do with that. What about Phil? The marshmallow as murderer? Or Alida? The kid's mother trying to murder me? That was easier to believe, but probably just because I didn't much like Alida. And I certainly didn't know how to tie Alida to Rick Clarence. Or John, if it came to that.

Was there another possibility? Could someone have overheard me talking to Alida? Could someone have simply recognized my car, seen it parked in back of the sheriff's office and gotten nervous? Why?

The only thing worse than waiting back at the ranch for the boys to come home was waiting back at the ranch while someone might be trying to kill me. And that deputy wasn't going to do anything to help. It appeared that I was going to have to take a trip to Davis, to find out what Rick Clarence was doing in Santa Clarissa. Besides, I would probably be safer somewhere else, not hanging around here waiting for my car to be fixed.

So what did I want to do about John? Oh, hell, I wanted to see him. Knowing it was a lousy idea, I still wanted to see him.

I dragged myself out of the tub and went downstairs to call him.

He wasn't happy when I told him about the car. Before I could finish, he interrupted.

"Why didn't you come here?"

"What?"

"Why are you at the inn? If you're in trouble, you should have come here. How long will it take you to pack and check out? I'll send Derek for you."

"I have a car—Russ Cahill drove me to Santa Barbara."

"Fine. How soon shall I expect you?"

"I haven't said I'm coming."

"What?"

"We missed a step here. I haven't agreed to come."

Silence. I started counting the beats. One, two, three. Then he broke it.

"Morgan, please stay here. I'd like you to."

"Thanks, John. I'd love to. I'll be there in about an hour."

It took me just over an hour—including leaving a note for Russ explaining my absence in case he actually did stop by the hotel the next morning. I didn't feel like calling the Cahill Winery. His mother might answer. Too much to explain.

John was waiting for me, out of the house before the engine died. He pulled my bags out of the car.

130

"I want to hear the whole story—including why Russ Cahill drove you to Santa Barbara!"

I followed him to the house. Normally, I would have tried to carry my own bags, but I was in enough pain that I decided not to argue.

He stopped at the door. "You're having trouble walking. Are you hurt? You should probably see a doctor. I know a good one in Santa Barbara. We can call him."

"I'm not hurt. I'm stiff. Russ took me horseback riding this morning. I don't need a doctor."

We glared at each other. This time I broke it.

"Really, I'm okay. A little scared, but okay."

"Okay."

I followed him through the living room, through his office, into a large bedroom dominated by a king-size bed with a white quilt that reminded me very much of the one in his penthouse, except that this time the view from the windowed wall was green, all hillside and staked vines.

On a marble-topped table beside the bed was a tray with a silver ice bucket containing a bottle of champagne. John dropped my bags.

"You've had a tough day," he said softly. "You might want to rest for a while before dinner."

"I might," I answered, caught again by the deep blue eyes.

He opened the bottle of champagne. "Would you like me to rub your back?"

"Oh, God, yes," I sighed. "And my thighs, please, my thighs."

I was out of my clothes before he had filled the two flutes. He handed me one and caressed it with his.

"To you. I've thought about you. I'm glad you're here."

"Yeah. Me too."

A bottle of lotion magically appeared. Just as magically, my muscles began to relax in his hands. I was drowsy, and I thought he had stopped, but then I realized he was just taking off his clothes.

131

"I'm truly glad I'm here," I said as I held out my arms to him.

I loved the way his skin felt in my hands, his lower lip in my mouth. The scent of his body, the dark side of jasmine. Rippling my hands through his thick white hair. The definition of his spine. The ease, the lack of urgency with which he slid into me, belied by the groan. My thighs circled him, pain forgotten.

In a long and checkered sexual career, there had been very few times—only with two other men and mostly under the influence of psychedelic drugs—when I had experienced the feeling of melting into someone else, the feeling of flesh giving way, of floating, spirit to spirit, transcendent, ego death, and ultimate rebirth. I floated into John that way, not caring for that instant whether I could return to self.

I returned when I felt compelled, afterward, to reestablish my own boundaries, to break the rhythm of my breath with his, to crack the water seal of our sweat. I reached for my champagne flute. Not quite willing to sever the cord completely, I poured the sip from my mouth to his, and took a second one for myself.

"Jesus," he whispered.

I snuggled back against him, face buried in the hollow of his neck, unwilling to talk about what I was feeling. I chuckled to myself. I simply didn't know him well enough.

And then it was broken. I opened my eyes and looked at him, realized that his had never been closed. We regarded each other for a moment.

"I'm going to have to get up," he said.

I stroked his belly, feeling the ridges of muscle, lingering on the indentation at his navel, examining his pubic hairs with my fingers. I didn't want this man to be a murderer.

"Why?"

"Because the day is not over, and while I would like to end it with you, I have other things to do first." He kissed me lightly. "Stay here as long as you like. Why don't you sleep for a while?"

132

"I may do that. Will you be close?"

"In the next room."

When I woke, the light was softer. I stretched, moved around in the bed, feeling the textures of the sheets and the quilt and the mattress, feeling the dampness our bodies had left, sniffing for the scent of sex.

I knew I was going to have to move, if only as far as the bathroom. But it was surely time to get up. My body disagreed. When I put weight on them, my thighs cramped immediately. Another bath was in order.

There was an adjoining bathroom, with a sunken tub and a recessed shower, all in Spanish tile. A large stained-glass window displayed a spray of green and white lilies of the valley. Fluffy brown towels were hanging on an oversize towel rack. One had been tossed back carelessly, probably the one John had just used. I couldn't catch his scent on it. I dried slowly, rubbed lotion into my skin, repaired my makeup, brushed my hair. His bathrobe was hanging on the back of the door, tan silk. I slipped into it.

I opened the door connecting the bedroom with the office, pleased to see him at his desk, Ben Franklin glasses low on his nose, peering at the paper in his hand.

"Hi," I said. "I'm up, and I feel great, I want you to know that."

He glanced up over his glasses.

"Oh, Morgan. Have you met my daughter, Francesca?"

I followed his gaze. I hadn't noticed that there was a smaller desk in the corner of the room, with an IBM PC and a printer taking up most of the space. A frozen Francesca was sitting there, turned awkwardly away from the screen, staring at me.

"Yes, actually, we did meet," I said uncomfortably.

"Yes, we did," Francesca said, still staring.

"Good to see you again, Francesca."

"Yes."

"Well, I guess I better put some clothes on," I said, as

lightly as I could. I pulled the door shut. He should have handled things better. But maybe he just hadn't thought.

When I had dressed—a white jumpsuit and my beloved pink sandals—and returned, Francesca had left.

"Hi," I said dryly, from the doorway.

"I'm sorry," he said. "It was foolish of me not to warn her that you were here. My only excuse is that I never invite women here, and I hadn't realized how much it would upset her. Please forgive me for embarrassing you."

"I forgive you. But maybe I shouldn't stay. I don't want to create difficulties for you."

"No, I want you to stay. As long as you like. Francesca really must learn to be a little less jealous of the women in my life. But if you don't mind, I think we should move your bags to the guest bedroom."

"I don't mind." I did mind, but I understood. I also felt a twinge at the word "women."

"You still haven't told me the whole story about your accident. And I do want to hear it. I'm sure the champagne is still chilled, but if not, we'll open another bottle."

The champagne was still cold. He dumped what was left in his flute in the bathroom sink—causing my Scotch-Irish heart to skip a beat—and rinsed both flutes in cold water before refilling them. We moved to the small patio outside the bedroom, shaded by the green hill behind the house. The furniture was redwood and padded, and he let me share his chaise and lean against him as I talked.

He was silent for a moment when I finished.

"I could make an argument on both sides," he finally said. "But this second accident—my gut feeling is that you're right. Someone killed Will and tried to kill you. So I want you to stay here until this is settled. Tomorrow, I'll check to see what the authorities are doing. If necessary, I'll hire a private investigator. But I think you should consider yourself off the case."

"What?" I lifted my head from his shoulder so that I could look at him. "Okay—I admit all this has distracted me from what I was supposed to be doing up here. So if you can get the police to take this seriously, it's fine with me. But tomorrow I talk with Cindy Frawn and maybe Henri Cheverin, both things I planned to do today. And then I head on to Davis. I still have an article on wine to write. I haven't really started it—which is really embarrassing—and I have a deadline." I decided not to mention that I could adjust my deadline. Not to mention that one of the few things I hated more than being pushed was being patronized. Not to mention that I still didn't know if John had a motive for murder.

"Why do you want to talk with Henri Cheverin?" He was suddenly cold, his eyes icy.

"I understand he's one of the more prominent winemakers. Of course I have to talk with him. What's wrong?"

"Nothing. Morgan, I think it's important that you stay here," he said calmly.

I wasn't sure if there was an undertone in his voice. If that was a threat.

"I just can't, John," I said. "I just can't do that."

I thought for a moment that he was going to lose his temper, and I braced myself for his fury. But he didn't. I watched him will his tension away, will himself to relax. And when he smiled, he seemed to mean it.

"You are stubborn, opinionated, and arrogant. Is there anything I can say to make you change your mind?"

"No," I said, sounding braver than I felt. "There really isn't."

"Then I won't try. And now we have an important decision to make."

"Oh?"

"Yes. We have to decide whether we're going to have dinner here, or go out. I had planned to have dinner with Francesca and Tony tonight, but if you'd rather go out, we can do that."

"What you're saying is that you don't want me to be uncomfortable."

"Yes."

"That's really sweet. I appreciate that. I feel fine about having dinner here, but how will Francesca take it?"

"She would probably rather you stayed than that we both left."

"Okay. Then we stay." I paused, then chuckled. "Who cooks?"

"Francesca, Derek, and Lucy work that out. I don't interfere. Francesca is really a superb cook, and my guess is that we'll see her hand in whatever we have tonight." He refilled our glasses, emptying the bottle. "I just realized how difficult it will be, having you here but in another bedroom."

"Well, probably you know how to find me if you want me," I said, thinking I was glad it would only be for one night. He was right, it would be difficult.

"Yes. Now perhaps we should join the others."

Tony was delighted to see me. He and Francesca were on what I had come to think of as Tony's Patio. Francesca was something less than delighted, but she had recovered her self-possession and put on a good show of civility, if not warmth. She had changed into a simple skirt and blouse of a soft mustard cotton. And she was now wearing makeup. I was surprised at how pretty Francesca was, not just young and fresh as I had originally thought. I thought how spectacularly beautiful Eva could be, if she wanted.

They were all willing to talk about the winery, which made the evening a productive one, if still a little tense. Francesca relaxed a little, but never totally gave up her hostility, despite the full blast of whatever charm I possess. She volunteered several stories that would add color to the article, including one about modern scarecrows—helium balloons shaped like hawks—that she had set out to keep the birds away from the sweet Chardonnay grapes. When the birds discovered the ruse, they pecked the "hawks" to death.

We moved inside for dinner, Lucy wheeling Tony. The table was set in the large living area, next to the French doors. And it was formally set—china, crystal, and silver on a linen cloth. Salads for the four of us were already in place, avocado

136

and orange slices with red onion arranged on a bed of greens and drizzled with a tart, creamy dressing. A basket of warm, sourdough rolls was also on the table, and an open bottle of Chardonnay sat in a cooler. The filtered gray light from the French doors was enhanced by an elaborate silver candelabrum, with white candles flaming gently.

Francesca clearly enjoyed her role as hostess. She had placed me at Tony's right, not John's.

I wondered if Lucy and Derek always ate separately, or whether it was just because they had a guest for dinner. I thought how lonely it must be for Francesca, with John away so much, and understood why she wanted him to herself on those rare evenings when he dined with them.

Derek silently cleared away the salad plates in the middle of Tony's scene-by-scene description of *The Barkleys of Broadway*, which he had seen on television the night before.

"I wish I could dance with you, Morgan. I'd like to dance with you the way Fred danced with Ginger," Tony said, his blue eyes filling.

"I'd like that, too, Tony," I answered, squeezing his hand.

Derek silently returned with the main course, chicken breast fillets poached in white wine with tarragon, rice, and a display of fanned pea pods and baby carrots. A dinner that Tony could cut with a fork, eat with one hand. I wanted to acknowledge Derek's presence, but no one else seemed to. He was like a prop man in a Chinese play, dressed in black so the audience didn't see him.

I was glad that I had agreed to have dinner in, since Francesca had obviously gone to a lot of trouble—for John, I knew, not for me. And I was glad that I could gush honestly about Francesca's culinary skills. She seemed pleased by the applause.

"Save room for dessert," was all she said, however.

Dessert was a dark chocolate soufflé, emerging triumphant from the kitchen at the proper moment, light and moist and bittersweet, served with barely sweetened whipped cream. All from Derek's invisible hands.

If I lived with Francesca, I would never cook again. But if she always cooked this way, I would weigh two hundred pounds, just from eating chocolate soufflé.

We lingered over coffee, too full to move. Shortly after Derek cleared the table, Lucy came in and started to wheel Tony away.

"Say good night to everyone," she said cheerfully.

"Not yet," he said sharply, the strong voice momentarily back. "I want to stay."

Lucy faltered, surprised. "Well, for a little while," she said, backing her way to the kitchen.

"Good for you, Tony," John said softly.

"Yeah," Tony said, pleased with himself, his wide blue eyes shining. "Yeah. Oh, this has been such a good evening. This has been the best evening I've had in a long time. Will you be here tomorrow night, Morgan?"

I hesitated. "I don't think so, Tony. I plan on leaving in the morning." I couldn't stand the way his face fell. "But maybe we could have breakfast together."

"Okay," he said, brightening a little. "I'd like that. And I understand that you have things to do."

No guilt, I thought, no guilt. "I hope I can take a rain check on that dinner."

"Yes," he said, his voice a whisper again. "Of course. Another time. Any time. I'm always here, you know."

The conversation never quite got going again, although John did his best to play the perfect host. It wasn't long before Tony decided that he ought to go to bed. Francesca wheeled him out of the room, rather than calling for Lucy.

"You're a hit," John said when we were alone.

"With part of the family, anyway."

"You mustn't take Francesca's reaction personally."

"I don't." We were silent for a while, in the near darkness of the dying candles. "Why is Tony always here? I know he's in a wheelchair, but is there some reason why he can't go anywhere?"

138

"No. I suppose he doesn't go anywhere because he never asks and no one ever volunteers."

"Would you mind if I took him out sometime?"

"Of course not."

"I'd have to borrow the Cadillac. I couldn't get his wheelchair in the trunk of the Alfa. Or even the Ford Escort."

"I'll be in New York next week. If you like, you can borrow Derek as well."

"I think I could manage, but I'll accept Derek's help gratefully. Will Francesca mind?"

"Probably. She's not as possessive of Tony as she is of me, however. And it would mean a lot to him. I think you should go ahead, if it's really something you'd like to do."

"It is. Couldn't he get around better if he had a motorized wheelchair?"

"His wheelchair is motorized. He likes to be pushed."

The silence fell again.

"You haven't said anything about my book-in-progress. Did you not read it, or did you hate it a lot?"

"I haven't read it. I didn't think I'd see you this quickly, and I've had other things on my mind. I do want to read it, and I will before the next time I see you."

Whenever that is, I thought. "Okay," I said.

The silence was longer.

"I wish you didn't have to sleep in the guest room."

"Yeah, me too."

The bedroom that he showed me to was nice enough. Probably better than my room at the Mission Inn, if one looked at it objectively. A queen-size brass bed with a peach down comforter, which I wouldn't need. Peach drapes. Oak dresser, and a truly fascinating oak wardrobe that I would have to look at in the morning. Someone (Lucy?) had unpacked my bags, a waste since I was just going to have to pack them again.

At the Mission Inn I wouldn't have had to share a bathroom with Francesca.

John's good-night kiss was polite, as if he were afraid some-

139

one might catch us, but it was just enough to make me want more, and I was glad I had a book to finish.

Still, I was restless in the night. I wasn't comfortable in the bed, in the house. And sometime in the night—I wished I'd had a watch, to know what time it was—I heard a car. Looking out the window, I saw the Cadillac pulling out.

When I returned to bed, I felt distinctly uneasy. And I missed my cats.

10

I managed to make my escape around eleven. Lucy woke me at eight, tap-tapping on the door to let me know that Tony was waiting for me and breakfast. John had already left. I knew that, but I didn't tell Lucy. Francesca had decided not to eat. I was bothered about John's midnight departure, relieved that Francesca was pouting. I ate more food than I wanted, to please Tony. And drank an extra cup of coffee, so that I was wired when I drove off.

Mornings in Santa Clarissa always made me feel momentarily as if this were the first day of vacation. My heart sang, I felt happy and lucky. I breathed deeply of clear air and sunlight. I wondered if it would be possible to spend my life feeling this way, waking this joyfully. Probably not. Reality would intrude, at some point, as it did when I thought about why I was there and what I had to do.

I pondered the questions as I drove off in the silly red Ford

Escort, wishing I had the Alfa with the top down in the sunshine.

I stopped at the garage, to see if any progress had been made. None. They didn't know when they would have the parts. I asked the question I should have asked the day before.

"Could someone have tampered with the wheel?"

"What?"

Why was it that no one around here seemed to hear my questions the first time I asked them? I repeated the question.

"Yeah, I suppose somebody could've," the mechanic said in a tone that was as close to thoughtful as he could get. "Somebody who knew what he was doing, maybe could've punctured the drum, put sand or something in to soak up the grease. Given time, just the air would've dried it out."

"Could you tell by looking at it?"

"Hard, you know, because of the damage, sharp rocks and all. But I'll see."

"Thanks. I'll check back with you in a day or two."

From the old Superman-booth pay phone, I put in a credit card call to Davis, asking for Vincent Perry. I might as well find out when I could see him before I drove up there. His office phone didn't answer, and when it didn't revert to the switchboard, I had to call back, making sure the university operator understood that I wanted to talk to someone in the office this time.

The third secretary informed me that Professor Perry wasn't there. After much prodding, she offered the further information that he was giving an intensive week-long seminar at Los Angeles University, and would be back the following Wednesday.

I almost shrieked with joy. Not Davis, but home! Cindy Frawn, Henri Cheverin, and then home!

I headed north into the hills, retracing my path of two days earlier. I pulled over and stopped when I saw the skid marks. I thought of Mark, the former owner of the Ferrari jacket, who had told me so many times that accidents happen because people hit the brakes when they should have hit the gas, and I silently blessed him, wherever he was. If I had hit the brakes, I would have spun out, lost control, and the car—even one with as low a center of gravity as the Alfa—might have flipped. With that sheer drop down the side, I would have been dead. Seat belt or not, although I never wore one because they made me feel claustrophobic. I sat there beside the bush where I had stopped—my bush—feeling cold in the sunshine, the way I had when we found the corpse in the wine cellar.

I wished I were home with my cats and my computer. If I could arrange all this into neat little data files, it might make sense to me. And once I figured it out, then I could get back to work on the article I owed Fred. I was feeling increasingly guilty about that article. Home soon. Back to work.

Cindy Frawn was pulling tiny weeds away from the roots of a giant zucchini plant when I found her. She looked once more the image of the hippie Cinderella, wearing a red cotton skirt and a gauzy red Mexican blouse, hair floating around her.

"I don't know what I'm going to do," she said. "The zucchini has just gone wild this year. I've made fried zucchini, stuffed zucchini, zucchini casserole, zucchini bread, zucchini cookies, zucchini soup, zucchini relish, zucchini preserves. Do you like zucchini?"

"Sure, doesn't everyone?"

"Good, I'll give you some before you go. Do you have any good recipes?"

"How about simply sautéed in olive oil with garlic and rosemary, then tossed with pasta and parmesan and a lot of black pepper?"

"That sounds great. Thanks. Come on in, and let's have some tea. How's your car?"

"Still in two pieces," I said, following Cindy toward the shed that served as home.

Tessa appeared from somewhere, dancing up, sun glinting on her silver coat, to sniff me and say hello.

As I walked inside, I felt the calm again, felt myself em-

143

braced by a peaceful presence. Someone had done a lot of work in this house. Sunlight streamed in, heightening all the colors, from windows in three sides. It occurred to me that the house was probably energy efficient, as well as energy giving.

"Solar collectors," I said. "I didn't look for solar collectors."

Cindy giggled, a shivery, little-girl giggle. She turned to me, her wide eyes shining. "You're picking up on the energy here, aren't you?"

"Well, yes. Doesn't everyone?"

"Not really, although a lot of people do. Ernie and I are really in a good place, and you can feel it in the house, that's all."

"You don't meditate under pyramids, or anything like that?"

Cindy giggled again. "Not exactly. I cast an occasional candle spell for harmony in the house."

"Are you a student of the occult?"

"You mean am I into witchcraft?"

This time I giggled with her. "Yeah."

"No, I just like to make things grow. I don't get into any of the other stuff."

"How long have you been here?"

"Six years."

"Six years? And you're still on your honeymoon?"

Cindy poured the boiling water into a heavy earthenware teapot, brought the pot and the cups to the table.

"I have to say not exactly, and it feels funny, as if nothing you're asking me is quite the right question, so I keep saying no, and I don't like saying no to people."

"Do you know what the right question is?"

"No, but you do."

"Oh, God, I don't. If I knew, I'd ask it."

"Then we have to find out. What do you really want to know?"

I paused, needing to sort that out. "Several things. I want to know who you are, how it happened that you lead such a happy life, and if it really is as happy as it seems. I want to

144

know about this valley, about winemaking, and particularly about John Novelli. I want to know if you have any information that would help me figure out who killed Rick Clarence and Will Baca and tried to kill me."

Cindy looked down. Tessa trotted over to her, and Cindy hugged the dog for a moment before she replied.

"I thought Will had an accident," she finally said. "I thought you had one, too."

I told her why I believed they weren't accidents. Cindy was silent for a moment longer.

"I'll start with your first question. I am what you see. Yes, I'm happy. This is the life I wanted, the life I imagined. I haven't always had it. When I met Ernie, I was still living in San Francisco, suffering a drugged hangover from my sixties dreams, working as a bookkeeper for a wholesale grocer. Ernie was the manager of a branch of a discount liquor store. We started talking because that was where I bought wine, and we found out we wanted the same things, we had the same secret fantasies of what we wanted to do when we were grown up, never mind that we were already grown up."

"How old are you?" I interjected.

"Thirty-six."

"That's my age—and about ten years more than I would have guessed."

"I know, but that's because I've never really grown up. You haven't either, so you understand. As far as I'm concerned, I'll always be eighteen."

"I do understand. I was nineteen for a long time, but I had a couple of bad years, and I think I'm up to about twenty-four. Although we have to wonder what kind of a compliment it is to be told that we don't look our age."

"Yes. I'm glad I'm starting to say yes to you. I like you better that way."

"Yeah, me too."

"To finish the first question as best I can, we're happy because we agreed on the kind of life that we wanted, we worked hard to get it, and we work very hard at keeping it.

It's on purpose, not by accident, that our life works. As far as your second question is concerned, I could probably tell you a lot about the valley, about seasons, and the changes in the air and the soil, and feeding the chickens and fertilizing the vegetables and testing the sugar level of the grapes, and I don't think that's what you want."

"It is what I want. It's what I need for the article I'm writing."

Cindy nodded. "But you don't want it right now."

I was feeling guilty again. "You're right. I haven't been doing a good job on the article, with everything else going on."

"About John, I don't know much. He asked me to have dinner with him once, I said I was busy, and that was the end. Anything else would be gossip. I don't do their books because Francesca does them herself. They have their own computer."

"Do you do the others by hand?"

"No. We decided to make one shed the office, so we had a separation of business and home. We keep the computer there."

"That makes sense."

"Yes. And that brings us to Rick Clarence. I did know Rick—I knew him in San Francisco. But I don't know anything about the rest of it."

"How well did you know him?"

"Well. Before I met Ernie. We were lovers."

"What?" I almost spilled my tea and was forced to set the cup down.

"Why are you so surprised?"

"I didn't know he was bi. I guess I *haven't* been asking the right questions."

Cindy's cup clattered to the floor.

"I don't understand. What do you mean?"

"Rick Clarence—the Rick Clarence found dead in the Novelli Winery last week—was identified by Phil Grademon—identified as his former lover."

146

"Oh, God. So that was it." Cindy started to rock back and forth in her chair. "So that was it."

"That was what?"

"What he couldn't tell me. I didn't ever know what it was, you know, why he left me." Her eyes became wild as they filled with tears. "I didn't even think anything about it when Phil identified him. I figured he'd met Phil on business or something."

"I understand," I said, but I wasn't sure I did. I realized— with some embarrassment—that I had been imagining this as a straightforward problem, with a simple solution, one that lay close to the Novellis. It hadn't occurred to me that the answer might lie with Rick's other lives in other cities. "Do you want to tell me the story?"

"I don't know. Sort of not, because it's a story about someone I'm not anymore, you know?"

"I know. But I'd like to hear about the person you were then."

"I was what I guess you'd call a flower child. I strung beads and played the guitar and did a lot of drugs and slept with a lot of men. I still play the guitar, though. I went to San Francisco State for a couple of years, but I never went to class very much. I demonstrated for peace and everything, and I really cared, but I was never one of the organizers, or anything like that. When I dropped out of school, I sort of drifted from job to job, the same way I drifted from man to man. I met Rick when I worked in the office at his company as a temporary typist. He was this scientist, you know, really serious about his work, there all the time. And really good-looking, too. He had blond hair, and a smile like an angel. I started getting there early in the morning so I could make coffee for him. And then I started bringing him things to eat, things I baked. He wanted to know about me, he really wanted to know who I was."

Cindy's face twisted, and she started to cry. I was reminded uncomfortably of Phil Grademon.

"Are you okay?" I asked, feeling stupid as I did so.

"I'm not sure," Cindy said sobbing. "I'm not sure I'm okay, but I'm so glad I can talk about this, it's been so hard not talking, since he died." The sobs choked her words off.

I moved over so I could hold Cindy as she cried. I cradled her in my arms, rocked her, as I would a child. The great, gasping sobs continued for a long time. When they subsided, Cindy continued, still leaning against me, wanting to be held.

"He was really concerned when my job ended, wanted to know what I was going to do next. It upset him that I didn't know. He wanted to keep seeing me, and I wanted that, too, you know? He kind of guided me, talked to me about getting skills to earn a living, getting off drugs, and it was really a long time—a couple of weeks or so after I left the job—before we made love. I wanted it so much, more than he did, I knew that. I wanted to get it together for him, even though I hadn't cared about doing it for myself, and so I started making plans about what I could do. And he stayed with me, until I got a regular job, until I really felt confident. Then he ended it. He disappeared out of my life. He wouldn't even return my phone calls. And I didn't know what else to do, so I kept going."

"When did you meet Ernie?"

"About six months later, but it was another year before we moved in together."

"Did you hear from Rick after that?"

"No. I read about him sometimes, though. It was in the newspapers, the work he was doing. So I knew where he was, when he went back to Davis. But I hadn't thought about him in a long time, until I read about him in the paper again, when he was identified."

"Then you don't know why anybody here would want to kill him?"

"No. I don't know why anybody anywhere would want to kill him." Her eyes brimmed again.

"Do you know why anybody here might have had business with him? Is there anything you can think of that might help, anything that might help me find out who he was seeing, or why he was here?"

"No. No, no, no. I don't know anything, except I loved him, and he left, and I started over, and I don't want to hear any more!"

She clung to my shoulder, sobbing. I waited until she wanted to continue.

"Rick was gentle, and generous, and honest, and he believed in what he was doing," Cindy said quietly, with a strength she hadn't had earlier. "He wanted to make a difference in the world. It just isn't right to kill someone like that."

Cindy sat up straight. After a moment, she got a paper towel and mopped up her spilled tea. She refilled our tea cups.

"I wanted to die when he left me, but it was like it would have been betraying him if I died, so I didn't. And at first I didn't want to stop hurting, because it seemed as if that would be betraying him, because it would mean forgetting him, but then when I kept going, I sort of wrapped him up in gold and hid him away, so he would be mine forever. And then when he was dead—I didn't know what to do. The thing wrapped in gold was like this bleeding lump in my heart, and I'm fine now, and I'm happy now, but I still hurt for him, and I weep for what he could have been, and what he could have done. I weep for what he can't give to other people now, that he gave to me. So I'm rewrapping that love in gold, and wiping the blood away, and I hope he knows whatever he did that hurt, I forgive him—I already forgave him a long time ago—and I just love him, and I want him to be okay and to go on and I want him to have better karma next time, and be happy."

Tears streamed down Cindy's face. I could smell the sweat that drenched her clothes. I was doing the best I could to handle my own stress, and now I was dealing with Cindy's as well. I waited as long as I could before I said it. "I don't suppose you have any Valium."

Fortunately, Cindy giggled. "No, I'm sorry. The best that I

can offer you is herb tea." She held out her hand. "And my thanks for being here."

"I don't see how you can mean that."

"You mean because of what you told me?"

"Yes."

"No, it's okay. I needed to hear that. I needed to know why he didn't love me, when I loved him so much." Cindy started to choke again, but this time she controlled it.

We sat, holding hands and sipping herb tea, until we both felt stabilized. I asked if I could come back another time. She said I could.

We sipped tea and held hands a while longer, then I left.

I drove on, farther into the valley than I had driven before, turning inland, watching the land become greener, flatter, the brown hills disappear. I couldn't fit the new picture of Rick Clarence into the puzzle.

The wineries I had been visiting were small, intimate. They hadn't prepared me for the Lindale Winery. It looked like a factory in the middle of the fields. No movie-set Spanish, no work-in-progress, no Haight-Ashbury revisited. This was cold steel, and I didn't want the tour.

I knew sooner or later I would have to take it. The Lindales had ten times the output of any other winery in the valley, and I would have to see what they were doing. Not today, though. I didn't even want to brave the tasting room, but I didn't know where else to start.

There were maybe twenty people milling around the counter, being served by three fresh-faced teenage girls and an equally fresh-faced boy who were probably all on summer vacation from Davis. I caught the attention of one of the girls, and explained I was looking for Henri Cheverin.

"He's in San Francisco, arranging for a charity wine tasting," the girl told me. "He'll be back on Friday. Could anyone else help you?"

No. No one else could help me. Not there.

The Ford Escort was an unsatisfying car, but I was willing to put up with it because I was going home. I whistled and chuckled and hummed to myself, even through the Santa Barbara gridlock. With the windows open and the radio tuned loudly to Pachelbel, with the sun on the ocean, with God in Her heaven (never mind that all was not right with the world), I could make it.

Nobody came to greet me as I drove into the garage. The Ford was an unfamiliar sound.

"I'm back," I yelled, walking up the steps, lugging my bags, the mail tossed in my purse. "Where is everybody?"

Chandra was sitting in a pot of impatiens, where the walk rounded the house, staring at me. No wonder the plant was dying, but it would do no good to tell Chandra that. Bubba peered at me from behind a rose bush. Salome stalked across a mess of scattered bird seed on the porch, squawking excitedly. Marcia came barreling from the backyard, screaming, butted my leg, and almost tripped me.

I disconnected the alarm, unlocked the door, and dropped my bags. Blaze, sound asleep on the sofa until the commotion started, glared at me for disturbing him, stretched and resettled himself.

I looked at the mail. Sallie Mae wanted to reduce my monthly student loan payments by stretching the payment period and incidentally raising the interest rate. Two banks wanted to issue me new credit cards, never mind my tenuous financial situation. An envelope with a famous TV star's return address (which I ripped open so eagerly that I suffered a paper cut on my index finger) turned out to be an appeal for funds from the L.A.U. Alumni Association. A grocery store, a hardware store, and a fast-food chain all enticed me with cents-off coupons.

Of the five messages on the answering machine, two were hang-ups. One was an encouraging message from Fred, hoping the article was going well, one was Tom, and one was John, sounding distraught.

I called John.

"Thank God," he said.

"What?"

"Morgan, there was an accident this afternoon. On the road that connects Los Robles with 101—the road you would have taken to Davis. A woman in a red Ford Escort went off the road. I found out it wasn't you, but I still wanted to know that you were all right."

"Is she?"

He hesitated. "No."

"Oh. I'm sorry. Who was it?"

"A woman who ran a bakery in Solvang, according to the reports. No one important."

"Oh." Who would have been important?

"I'm so glad you weren't hurt, that you didn't go to Davis after all. Where are you?"

Something in my solar plexus went crunch.

"I'm safe."

Was I? I had to think. It wasn't just my own safety. There were four cats and a peahen I was responsible for.

"John?"

"Yes?"

"I can't talk any longer right now. I'll call you tomorrow."

I hung up the phone and sat there shivering.

11

Elly had worked her way methodically through an open-faced sandwich while I told the story. The sandwich was colorful and attractive when served, with delicate slices of chicken breast interspersed with avocado on one thick piece of whole wheat bread, and tomatoes, cucumbers, and alfalfa sprouts on the other. Several ladles of Thousand Island dressing had turned it into an unappetizing speckled orange mass. I was doing more talking than eating, but had picked my way through part of a spinach salad.

We were sitting on the covered patio of the L.A.U. Faculty Club dining room. Because it was Friday, and summer, we had it almost to ourselves. This was my first visit in more than a year. The last had been under unfortunate circumstances, and I had wondered how I would feel, meeting Elly there. I discovered that—except for an allergy attack that responded immediately to decongestants—I felt fine.

Elly looked the best that I had ever seen her. Her hair was

no longer red. It was now a dark brown that made her skin look warmer. And—although there was no getting around the fact that Elly was fat—her body seemed more solid, less sloping. Maybe it was the cut of the checked coral and white jacket and pants, which gave Elly a dress-for-success appearance, despite the heat. Men do that, I thought. They dress-for-success no matter how hot it is. Some women do. I didn't. I was in a pale aqua sundress, showing off my tan.

The waiter, a young, smiling, clean-cut student in a white shirt and slacks, refilled our glasses of iced tea. Elly ordered a dish of chocolate mint ice cream and turned her attention back to me.

"Do you really think John is trying to kill you?"

"I don't know. I hope not. Oh God, I hope not. I just didn't want to tell him I was at home until I could decide. I almost made up a story about calling my machine from somewhere else and getting his message, but then I didn't want to do that. I just wanted to get off the phone. The thing is—if it wasn't John, who was it? Who knew I planned on going to Davis?"

"But then why would he tell you about the other woman's accident? Why would he put you on your guard?"

"Yes, thank you, I don't know why. None of it makes sense to me, and I don't know how I got into the middle of this."

"What are you going to do?"

"Work my way out of it, as best I can, and that means trying to find out who is behind all this. You know, I wanted so much to believe it wasn't John that I've never even asked him where he was when Rick was murdered. And now I'm afraid to. He did say he had the opportunity."

"But not the motive."

"What if he did? What if that's why he doesn't want me to talk to Henri Cheverin?"

"Well, you'll have to talk to Henri Cheverin and find out." Elly peered at me, small eyes made larger by her thick lenses. "Murder aside, how do you feel about him?"

"How can I answer that? How do you set murder aside?"

"I'll rephrase that. Let us assume for a moment that John

is indeed neither a murderer nor an attempted murderer, and that this assumption will be justified by the results of your investigation. How do you feel about him?"

"I'm fascinated by him. I like being with him."

"And he reminds you of Aaron Fisher, the dead love of your life."

"Yes. In some ways. Not in others. They're both white-haired, blue-eyed, suntanned womanizers. But there's something ruthless about John, something far colder than Aaron's self-absorption. And John's taller, heavier, and his face is harder. In fact, I think it's really only his hair that reminds me of Aaron, that white halo."

Elly made a face to indicate she didn't believe that for a minute. "Do you think this is going to result in some investigator bias?"

"Look, if Sam Spade can turn in Brigid O'Shaughnessy— hey, I can turn in John."

She just stared.

"Look," I continued, "there's always investigator bias, even in the hard sciences. And investigator bias is so endemic in all the sciences that no one can figure out why, in the social sciences, in experiment after experiment, women score significantly higher when the research is done by women than they do when the research is done by men."

Elly nodded. She knew that.

"But bias aside—the point is," I said, ignoring another face, "I need to know whether he did it. And if he didn't, who did. It's the only way I'll feel safe again."

"What about Tom?"

"What about him?"

"Two things occur to me. One is that not long ago you were heavily involved with him, and you seem to have dropped him rather abruptly. The other is that you'd be safe with him until this thing is solved."

"I was involved with him, true. Rebound from Aaron, pure and simple. And grief, and fear, and all that. But he really

155

wasn't an appropriate choice for anything more than a temporary sexual liaison."

"Reducing Tom to sociological jargon makes you sound
awfully detached."

"I know. I guess I am. Except I think I hurt him, and I'm
sorry about that. I need to call him and tell him, and I'm such
a coward I'm putting it off. Besides, he'd want to know what
was going on, and I don't want to get into it with him."

"Since you're labeling Tom, how would you label John?"

"A fascination that I don't really expect to last."

"Glib."

"I know. Getting back to 'safe'—as far as 'safe' is concerned, I don't want my safety, physical or emotional, to
depend on anyone else. 'Safe' has to come from me."

"Yes. And you keep yourself emotionally 'safe' by only
getting involved with men who aren't going to get too close to
you."

"Or women either. You're as close as anybody, and how
often do we see each other?"

"Are you really happy with intimacy on the run?"

"Most of the time I am. Especially when I think the alternative would be having somebody there all the time, demanding
things of me."

"What things?"

"I don't know. Cook dinner, do laundry, clean the house.
All the things my mother felt she had to do and hated doing,
all the things that kept her sighing all day long, the things that
drove her to drink. Did I tell you that she even ironed the
sheets?"

"Come on. None of that has to happen. Look at me. Steve
does the laundry, and most of the time he cooks dinner or we
eat pizza, and we hire somebody to clean the house."

"I know—you and Steve have the only good marriage I'm
aware of. And whenever I meet a new man I spend a day or
two—more often a night or two—thinking that this one might
be magic, this one might want to negotiate a relationship that
I could live with. And actually, I love to cook dinner, but only

156

occasionally and on my own terms. What always happens, though, is he—whoever he is—ends up wanting either too much or too little."

"And what do you do?"

"I either don't get involved at all, or I get involved a lot, and then I give in and give in and give in and wonder who needs this oppressive relationship anyway."

"And you go back to being alone—and 'safe.' "

"Yes. And that's what I have to work on right now. Making me safe. And to do that, I need to find out who Rick Clarence was planning to see, other people he might have *wanted* to see, and if any of them might have had a motive to murder him."

"You just switched 'safes' on me."

"I know. Don't you think I'm clever?"

"No. But I'll let it go. What next?"

"Next, I'll get what information I can from this Perry fellow—I used my wine article as an excuse to set up an appointment for this afternoon. And I still have Henri Cheverin to see. And then I'll decide what's next."

"Are you really scared? You don't appear to be."

"My body is terrified. So I have to stay in my head, which is remarkably calm—even without drugs. It is so calm that I can even point out that we've been talking for an hour and a half, and we've never gotten around to you. How's your kid?"

"Remarkably articulate for a three-year-old. I think his nursery school teacher is a little intimidated by him."

I was certain his nursery school teacher was intimidated by him. I imagined Elly's incisive mind in the body of a small boy built like a sumo wrestler. Elly talked about him a bit longer, explaining that he could already play his Sesame Street cassettes on the VCR, and that she expected him to be computer-literate by the time he was five.

After I left Elly, I had a few moments to stroll around the campus before it was time to meet Vincent Perry. It was still beautiful—cooled by the faint breeze in the jacaranda trees, brightened by unexpected beds of late-blooming purple pansies—especially at this time of year when it was almost deserted—not spoiled by the students, as the faculty would say. A couple of staff members smiled at me as if they almost but not quite recognized me. I didn't want to risk running into old friends and headed for the other side of campus.

Perry's temporary office was in the original natural science building, long since abandoned by L.A.U.'s heavily endowed professor-scientists for newer and flashier quarters. But I liked the old building, with its aged brick and gargoyles on the outside and its faded mosaic panels of seventeenth-century scientists inside, the only one of whom I could recognize was Isaac Newton.

I climbed to the third floor. The door had an opaque glass panel with the room number chipping off. Deferred maintenance strikes again. No one answered when I knocked. And the door was locked.

I had been waiting about ten minutes when a short man with a sweep of gray hair, wearing a green plaid sport shirt and gray slacks that hung from a waist too round for the rest of him, appeared. I didn't want to think that he minced to the door, because that sounded so stereotypical. But the truth was, he minced to the door. He looked at me from wide, long-lashed, hazel eyes, magnified by his thick glasses. Whatever was wrong with his eyes was close to what was wrong with Elly's.

"Are you the girl reporter?" he asked. His voice was high and thin, with a slight quaver.

"I'm the woman writer who called and asked for an appointment, yes," I replied, hoping that we weren't going to have an impossible task communicating.

He blinked and nodded, evidently unconcerned. He opened the door and motioned me in.

"I hope this won't take long," he said. "I really don't have very much time. The seminar resumes at three, and I want to go over my notes. Whenever I do that, I'm amazed at what interesting things I discover."

The office looked like a temporary office. An old desk with

158

a few papers on it, two old chairs, an old bookcase empty except for a few textbooks and some paperbacks. Perry sat down in the chair behind the desk. I took the one opposite. I looked past him, out the window with the opaque top pushed out like a skylight. The view was hazy sky, one I would have called light blue but clear before my last few days in Santa Clarissa.

"Did you know that if you prick a peeled peach ninety-nine times with a fork and drop it into a glass of chilled champagne it will revolve slowly?"

I recovered, smiled. "No, I didn't know that."

He nodded, as slowly and solemnly as the peach might revolve. "It's true. Try it sometime."

"I will. Is that in your notes?"

"Somewhere. I don't think it's in the notes for today, though."

The nods were almost hypnotic, and I began nodding in rhythm with him. I tried to think of questions I could ask about winemaking. I started to pull my notes out of my purse. Later.

"I have to tell you the real reason I'm here," I said, still nodding. "While it's true that I'm doing an article on wine, it's also true that I have some concerns over the murder of Rick Clarence."

He stared at me, never blinking as I repeated the same story I had told Elly—minus John.

"Did you check his calendar?" he asked.

"Yes—the two weeks leading up to his death were missing."

"Oh my, that's too bad. That would have given you the information you wanted about his appointments and his thoughts about those appointments as well, probably. The calendar defined Rick's present life. His past is more complicated, of course."

He stopped, and I didn't know what to say. Finally, he continued.

"For an apprentice winemaker, one of the most difficult

things to learn is how to take a sip of raw wine into one's mouth and sense the possibilities. And yet we do that with people—with young people, we take sips and sense their possibilities for growth, for developing, for becoming richer and more complicated as they age. We make the same kinds of judgments with people that we do with wine. The analogy breaks down, of course, because one always spits out the wine. And wine doesn't take it personally. Rick seemed sturdy. I was certain he was going to age well—and he was certainly complex—but I'm sometimes wrong about wine, too. Phil always had a strength of character, but he was unpretentious, and Rick couldn't perceive his beauty. I think part of it was that Phil loved him so much. It's hard sometimes to see the truth of someone who loves you that much. And Rick spit him out. Actually, I think Rick enjoyed spitting people out. Most of us don't, you know."

"I know." I had trouble imagining someone who enjoyed spitting people out. I didn't want to think about it. "I know something of Phil's story from Eva Novelli. I need to know about Rick—what did Rick do when he left Phil?"

"He moved to San Francisco. He became involved with some woman, and of course that didn't work. Professionally, he was doing some important things. He was a good scientist. Personally, he alternated between short, intense affairs, like bouts of drunkenness, sometimes with men, rarely with women, and periods of celibacy. He wasn't happy, and while he was intensely generous during those short, intense affairs, he certainly wasn't making anyone else happy. He finally moved back to Davis and devoted himself to his work."

"Did he make anyone unhappy enough to think of murder?"

"How unhappy is that?"

"I don't know—I guess it depends on character, doesn't it?"

"Yes. So the other thing you need to know is that there is at least one person in Santa Clarissa who was perhaps going to be very unhappy."

160

"Oh?"

"Phil has been living for the past several years with a young man, Michael Garth, his partner in the winery. Rick had planned to ask Phil to forgive him, to tell him that living with him was the only time he'd been happy, to talk about trying again. Would Phil have done it? I don't know, of course. Would Michael be afraid that he would? That is the more interesting question. Rick was brilliant and charming and persuasive and unprincipled. And Phil had once loved him very much."

"That's why you've told me all this. You think Michael might have killed him."

"I don't know. But I sense that no one is doing very much, and you seem to have an interest."

"Yes. Well. You said at least one person in Santa Clarissa. Do you know of anyone else who might have wanted him dead?"

"No, but that doesn't mean there isn't someone. He had been testing some Santa Clarissa wines, and he had reason to believe that someone had used pesticides on the grapes."

"Which winery?"

"I don't know. He didn't tell me that. He wanted to discuss it with whoever it was first. That kind of thing destroys reputations, you know. It would take years for a winery to recover from such an accusation."

"I'm sure it would." I knew it would.

We sat in silence, Perry unblinking, me fidgeting as I tried to think of something more to ask him. I stood and held out my hand.

"Thank you for the information."

"Please use it," he answered.

Could Michael be the killer? Which winery did Rick Clarence suspect? The obvious choice was the one where he was found, poisoned with a common pesticide.

I wanted to get home, back to my computer, check notes and make new ones. I made the mistake of thinking that the freeway would get me there faster than surface streets. There was an accident at the junction of the Santa Monica and Harbor freeways, and the six and a half miles took me an hour.

Home was ten degrees hotter than the yard—I could have baked bread in the living room, if I were still doing that, so my first task was opening the house and turning on the fans. I also had to check the herb garden. Norman hadn't given the little plants quite enough care while I had been gone, and I had almost lost a couple. I was watering them every day now.

The rosemary wasn't as vulnerable as the others. When I had discovered the kind of great, wonderful, fragrant bush that rosemary could become, I had decreed that two of the rosemary plants would not be touched for years—I would snip the other two only. The spared ones couldn't be called bushes yet, but they were obviously working at it, proud of the distinction. Unfortunately, Marcia loved the smell of rosemary and tended to nibble the plants, and I hadn't been able to explain to her that two should be left unnibbled.

By the time I fed the cats and opened a bottle of wine, my office was cooled to an almost bearable eighty degrees. The temperature was more bearable than the wine, in fact. What was going to happen to me if I lost the ability to tolerate inexpensive wine? Success was going to have to come fast, that was all.

I stripped to a blue silk teddy, tossed a clean towel over the rocking chair at the desk so that I wouldn't stain the cushions with perspiration (unlike the legendary Rita Hayworth, my glow was accompanied by a perceptible dampness). I felt the languor of the sauna creeping up on me, and fought the urge to take a nap. I booted up the computer, called up the Rick Clarence file, and opened a new file labeled SUSPECTS.

John Novelli. Eva Novelli. Francesca Novelli. Phil Grademon. Michael Garth. Alida Cahill. Cindy Frawn? I didn't want to do that, but I knew I had to. And what about the mysterious Henri Cheverin?

Means. Probably any of them had the means to poison Rick Clarence. All of them either had keys to the wine cellar or could have known about the one in the kitchen, and they all had access to parathion. Who knew enough about cars to sabotage Will Baca's? Or mine? Did John? John, of course, had an additional tool—Derek. Derek knew enough about cars. And while John might not want to get his hands dirty, he wouldn't have the same compunction about Derek's.

Opportunity. Phil was the only one who apparently had an alibi for Rick's murder. Although I hadn't been good about asking. Rick might easily have agreed to meet Eva or Michael. Or Cindy. John? Maybe, on business. (Something tugged at me here. There was something else that should go in here, that I was forgetting.) Alida? Same. Will's car could have been tampered with any time (as far as I knew), and everybody seemed available to tamper with mine. But one more time: Who besides John knew I was planning to go to Davis?

Motive. Michael Garth, jealousy. Phil Grademon, old pain, especially if he had killed Rick before Rick had a chance to tell him he wanted to come back. Not likely, that one, but who knew. Cindy, same, except Rick didn't want to come back. Eva, no motive that I knew of. John, Alida, preserve the reputation of their wines? John said he had no motive, but maybe he thought I wouldn't find out, maybe he just wanted to disarm me. How about pesticides at Polarity? Really unlikely. Same with Lindale, but think about it.

Who knew I thought Will's death suspicious—that was one more variable. John. Alida (and her kid). Eva. Cindy.

Maybe Will had figured it out. Did Will have the pages from the calendar? Were they torn out later? I leaned toward Michael. I wanted it to be Michael. He loved Phil, loved the winery, was afraid of losing both. Jealousy and fear were such nice motives, and the circumstantial evidence was so comfortable. But I still had an uncomfortable feeling that John was capable of dismissing a threat—permanently.

Who might know something about the wineries and be willing to talk? Cindy Frawn would, surely, if she wasn't guilty, and I had trouble thinking she might be. And there was another possibility. I looked in the Westside telephone directory under Novelli. The listing was there. Novelli, C. A. A Bel Air address.

Carla Novelli first said she had no comment about the Novelli Winery, but finally agreed to see me the next afternoon.

I invariably get lost in Bel Air, partly because I'm there so seldom. As soon as I drove between the crumbly white pillars called the Bel-Air Gate, I became disoriented. It was like Wonderland to me, the way whichever direction one turned was still Bellagio Road, or perhaps Bellagio Place. I headed up the hill, past piles of impatiens with bright, tiny flowers, red, white, and purple. Past great clumps of lilies of the Nile, growing wildly, reminding me of a sign I had once seen on a fence, BEWARE OF AGAPANTHUS. Here the signs all said ARMED RESPONSE. Past ivy, past bougainvillea, past cypress trees, all protecting the fences, the gates, the hidden houses, the hidden worlds behind the gates. Then a stretch with no houses, beside a canyon. The oddity of open brush in the middle of the urban area, something I could never get used to. I followed the road around the hill.

The driver of a car coming the other way on the narrow road started waving frantically at me. I slowed, rolled down the window.

"I'm looking for Mount St. Mary's College," he said.

"What?"

The driver's wife muttered something in an Asiatic language that I couldn't catch. He handed me a flier advertising a Bach concert at Mount St. Mary's College.

"Chalon Road is that way," I said, pointing in the direction the driver was headed. "I'm not sure which way you turn."

He nodded, whispered to his wife, drove off.

I hoped they found it, but had my doubts.

The first time I had been in Bel Air, meeting someone at the Hotel Bel-Air for lunch, I had felt as if I were Alice trying to get to the house—I could see it, but I couldn't figure out how to get there. And none of the roads had seemed to take me any closer. Finally, when I started to drive away, ready to ask the Red Queen for help, I had found myself at the door.

The door to the Novelli house was bleached wood, as was the trim. The rest of the house was some kind of weathered gray wood. The house was one story, L-shaped, with the base of the L stepping down the side of the hill. I had almost missed the driveway, the front of the property blended so well with the surrounding cypress trees and ivy. I drove down to a carport that held only one car at the moment, a dark green Jaguar, but could easily accommodate four.

A silent, white-uniformed Hispanic woman—almost Indian, with her long, straight, lusterless black hair and sullen features—met me at the door. She had that old look that young women get when nothing has ever gone right in their lives and they don't understand why.

The woman led me down three steps to a living room that looked out over the city. I wondered if John had always insisted on one glass wall, if every house he had ever lived in had one glass wall and a spectacular view. The stone fireplace, too, echoed the house in Santa Clarissa. And the hand that decorated this living room had the same taste. The huge curved sofa that embraced both the fireplace and part of the open wall was low and gray and soft, with a low gray marble table in front of it. But another hand had placed on the table—with duplicates almost everywhere else I looked in the room—a riotous display of fresh flowers, red and white and green, like a defiant Mexican flag, in a tall gray and white ceramic vase.

I walked to the windowed wall. For L.A., it wasn't smoggy. For anywhere else, it would be pretty bad. I was reminded of the definition of an Angeleno as someone who didn't trust air he couldn't see. The haze was more gray than brown, and I could sort of tell that the city was in a basin, even though I couldn't see mountains distinctly and had to intuit where the city ended and the ocean began. On truly clear days, one could probably see all the way to Catalina—the mark of an outstanding L.A. view.

"On clear days, you can see Catalina," a musical voice behind me said, "but there really aren't many clear days. I've tried to decide whether the air has been getting better or worse during the years I've lived here, but I can't. I think my opinion is influenced by my mood, how I feel about the city, so many things."

I turned and introduced myself to Carla Novelli. Whatever I had been expecting John's ex-wife to look like, and the image had never been clear for me, this was not it. Carla was a little shorter than I, and considerably heavier. She was a well-proportioned heavy, though, like a Renaissance nude, and she carried her weight with confidence. She wore a long lounge dress, Bullock's Wilshire Chinese, bright red silk that draped and flowed about her. Her face was straight out of *Big, Beautiful Woman*—clear, unlined skin (face lift? I wondered, as I searched the face for its resemblance to Eva's), huge brown eyes. Her hair, however, was grounds for *BBW*'s rejection. I remembered Eva saying that her mother had her hair done every week. It showed. Carla's hair was too dark, too thin, and too frizzed—in a word, overprocessed. Ox-eyed Hera, living alone on Olympus.

"Would you like something to drink?" Carla asked. "Iced tea, mineral water?"

I accepted mineral water, which the sullen maid brought in, deposited on the table. I told Carla as much of the story as I comfortably could, leaving out only the nature of my relationship with John. I knew that was a major omission, but I couldn't help it.

"What do you want from me?" Carla asked.

"I'm not sure I know exactly—I do know I want help."

"To prove John is innocent, or to prove he's guilty?"

We were sitting on the gray sofa, close enough to talk, far enough apart to show that there was no intimacy. Carla was settled comfortably. But the sofa was too low for me to be comfortable, or my legs were too long. There was no good place to put them. They were bent at an awkward angle, and

I was glad I hadn't worn a skirt. I had tried leaning back, legs out, and felt like a child. Now I felt perched.

"What do you mean?"

"Women aren't indifferent to John. They love him or they hate him, but they care. *You* care one way or the other. This thing—whatever it was—happened in Santa Clarissa, and you came to see me, so you want something from me about John, although you didn't say that directly. If you want my help, I have to know what I'm helping."

"I guess before I go on I need to know how you feel about him now—whether you'd rather see him innocent or guilty."

"I'd rather believe he's innocent of murder. After all, I lived with him for twenty-seven years. But I believe he's guilty of several other things, and I don't know how many of them are illegal." Carla paused, appraising me. "I can't remember when I first realized that he was seeing other women. I've tried, because I've thought that there must have been something special that gave him away. The first time he came home too late from a meeting and showered before he came to bed? The first time a woman with a faltering voice called the house and asked for him? The first time he went away for a weekend on business and made it clear that he didn't want me with him? The tenth time any of those things or so many others happened? I know it took a long time for me to realize, I know I was naive. I really hadn't wanted to know, of course. For years after, I was destroyed by that knowledge. Wherever we went, whatever woman smiled at me, I wondered what she knew, and I couldn't smile back."

She paused, smiling at me. But her voice was serious when she continued.

"And then I watched my daughter, Eva. I saw her at the beginning with Will, when she loved him so much, and realized that I had set the wrong example—I had taught her that he was to be her whole life, that she had to take it, whatever he did, whatever it did to her soul, that she had to give till it hurt, that she didn't deserve to be happy if this man, whatever man, didn't want to present happiness to her. I was

167

teaching my daughters, both of them, that they weren't responsible for their own lives. I had to change that. The only way I could think of was to leave John."

"But you must have wanted to leave him—for yourself."

"Not at the time. That came later. That came after I found out what it was like to be free. John thinks he paid for his freedom. I think I paid for mine. I love this house, but I live alone in it, and that was not what I imagined. Ultimately, my daughters were not mine, but his. And that was a terrible price to pay."

"Eva? You think Eva is his?"

"More than she realizes."

I would have to think about that. "You don't seem to hate him for it. I think I might."

Carla smiled, a tolerant, maternal smile. "Now you might. And at first I did. But then I set them free, too. All of them live their own lives, as I do. I'm here, if they need me. They think they don't. I stopped resenting that some time ago."

"And how do you feel about him now?" I didn't want to consider how I felt about him now.

"Detached. I remember loving him desperately, and I know that I'm the same woman, and he's the same man, and I haven't stopped caring about him. But the connection is gone, and I'm grateful for that."

"Okay. I want him to be innocent—it's really uncomfortable for me to think of him as a murderer—but if he's guilty, I can live with that."

Carla nodded. "You don't want to think you've slept with a murderer?"

"Not exactly." I flushed, remembering, not wanting to get into the issue of sex. "I've slept with men who've taken other men's lives, for one reason or another." A flash of Tom, which I dismissed. "I don't want to think I've slept with someone who would consider taking mine—and who could then lie to me about it so easily."

Carla nodded again. "Yes. I can understand that," she said calmly, so calmly that there had to be some underlying rage.

168

"He's not an honest man, and he does lie easily. And he can be a brutal man. He isn't too particular how he gets what he wants, as long as he gets it. Nevertheless, poisoning someone and leaving the body to be found in his own wine cellar doesn't sound like something he would do."

What if he had planned to move the body, though, get rid of it somehow, and then he couldn't? What if someone surprised him? I needed a deep breath. "Who *would* do that— who would poison someone and leave the body in John's wine cellar?"

"How can I answer that? Someone who wanted to cause problems for him—or someone who wasn't thinking of him at all, strange as that may seem to you now."

"Can you think of someone I could talk with, someone outside the family and maybe even outside the valley, who might have some information? On why someone might have used pesticides, if not why someone committed murder?"

"I can think of two people you might want to see," Carla said, after some consideration. "Henri Cheverin is the winemaker at Lindale Winery. He was the original winemaker at Novelli—Gordon Lindale hired him away."

"Yes, I heard part of that." Henri Cheverin again. "Is there some story behind that?"

Carla raised her already arched brows, displeased by the interruption. She continued. "I believe the Lindales made him an offer he couldn't refuse, as the saying goes. But I don't really know. If anyone knows what skeletons might be buried in the valley wineries, Henri would. The other is John's cousin, Theo. He's family, but not close. Theo had a small winery for a few years, but he got into some trouble and sold out. Something to do with speculating in wine futures."

"I didn't realize there was a futures market for wine."

"Oh, yes, my dear. Wine is bought and sold at all stages, sometimes even before it is quite wine, although I don't think they do that so much anymore." Carla laughed lightly, fluttering her long lashes, dark petals of her oxeyes. "Isn't it

169

amazing what you pick up from being there—even when you don't care?"

Don't you, I thought. "I can use my article to approach Henri. Why would Theo be willing to talk to me?"

"Theo and John had a falling-out when Theo sold his land to the Lindales. John wanted the acreage at a discount. Anything Theo has on John, he'll gladly tell to someone who might publish it. Besides, Theo likes attractive women—even more than John does."

"Do you really feel that adultery is John's worst sin?"

"No. But it's the only one that directly concerns me, and therefore the only one I'm willing to discuss."

That was it. Carla gave me Theo's address and phone number, and we parted politely. I got lost on my way back to the Bel Air Gate, and somehow ended up on the San Diego Freeway headed north, thinking it was south. I took the long way home.

Home was the usual flurry of feathers and fur. Salome preened, hoping for a second handful of cat food. Bubba went racing halfway up a tree beside the front porch, twitching his tail while he waited for me to open the door. Marcia screamed, Blaze glared. Chandra limped up on three paws, sat dangling one and staring accusingly.

"Well, what happened to you?" I asked, but Chandra continued to dangle her paw and stare accusingly.

Alarm off, fans on. I picked Chandra up to examine her paw, putting on my glasses to catch thorns or festering foxtails. Nothing. And Chandra didn't seem to be in pain. A sprain—the dumb cat had sprained her paw.

"Okay," I said. "You have two days to heal, and then we go to the vet to make sure it's a sprain, that you don't have something wrong that I missed. You understand?"

Chandra settled on my lap. The paw evidently worked when necessary.

The mail. An invitation to a New Age meditation group. A bill for a lavender and white silk suit that had called my name from clear across the store, guiding me unerringly to its rack.

"You'll wear it everywhere," the saleswoman had chanted. Another bill for a pale blue terrycloth bathrobe to replace my white one that had become so grungy from coffee stains and cat claws that I felt like a waif when I put it on in the morning. Another bill for the white belt that I needed for the silk suit. No more purchases this month, I vowed. No more purchases until I sold something. No more purchases until I finished my book, even. Except maybe a pair of lavender sandals, that would be nice. And I really needed a new pair of white sandals, too. Finally, a newspaper account of the winner of the annual Bulwer-Lytton contest, for most convoluted opening lines, sent from an old friend at L.A.U., in case I missed it. I chuckled, made a mental note to call him, catch up on old times.

The messages. Three hang-ups again, Fred had called again, and Tom had called again. I called the number Carla had given me for Theo, reached a machine, hung up, and decided to call back on Monday. I bit the bullet and called Tom.

"Why the hell haven't you returned my calls? I was about ready to drive to L.A. and camp on your doorstep."

"I haven't been here much. I'm sorry, I guess it was rude of me."

"I'm not sure I want to ask where you've been."

"Good."

"Oh, hell. Morgan, I don't know what it was I did that set you off, but I apologize for whatever it was."

"You didn't really do anything. It's me, it isn't you. I've told you. You want things from me, and there's nothing wrong with what you want, it's just that I don't want to give them. And there's so much tension between us over it that I don't have a good time with you anymore."

"Is that all you want? A good time?"

"That's cheap."

"Yeah, I'm sorry. But I don't want to give you up."

"But you have to give me up. You don't have me, don't you see that?"

"Listen, we shouldn't be having this discussion over the phone."

I thought about that. I didn't want to feel guilty. Nevertheless, I did.

"Okay. I'm coming up Tuesday. We can have dinner."

In my student days, I had a friend who would occasionally show up without warning, lean against my doorjamb and drawl, "Which would you rather do, walk barefoot through a Georgia swamp or go have a beer?"

To my automatic response, "Go have a beer," he would always smile and say, "Fine, let's go."

I would rather have walked barefoot through a Georgia swamp than have dinner with Tom to convince him that it was really over.

Dismissing Tom and my guilt, I booted up the computer. Having seen *2001* at an impressionable age, I had thought about naming the computer and decided that was weird. Like naming cars. I had named an MG once, but then I felt disloyal selling the car when the electrical system developed a phantom short. How could I have coped with the Alfa, disabled 150 miles away, if I had named it? Still, I felt a kind of affection for the computer.

I pulled up the Rick Clarence file again. What did I know? Damn little, but I had a lot of possibilities, just like everybody else in L.A. There were still people I hadn't talked to and people I could talk to again. I had made it through tough times when the odds had been against me, and I would make it through this.

The article—and worse, my book—would have to wait until I found out who was trying to kill me, and that was starting to annoy me a lot.

12

Theo Novelli answered the phone himself and agreed to see me—provided that I met him within an hour. I made it, but it meant that I had to rush. I didn't like rushing at the best of times, and truly resented it in the heat. Fortunately, his office was downtown, so transportation time wasn't a problem— although I almost blew it because I wasn't used to the new, one-way streets. I was going to have to take the urban planners' word that they helped the traffic flow. Downtown traffic always seemed to get worse, never better. But I lost my resentment in the thrill of being on time. I have the Los Angeles disease: I always underestimate how long it will take me to get where I'm going, and thus am usually about ten minutes late. Sometimes more.

If Theo had lost a bundle on wine futures, you couldn't tell it from his address. It was on the seventeenth floor of a brand-new skyscraper that boasted an ultramodern shopping mall on the ground floor, part of the program to revitalize downtown L.A. Tiny white lights blinked on globular open sculptures around the entrance, reminding me of artificial Christmas trees. Sandals, I thought as I walked in the main doors. I need lavender sandals. I forced myself to head straight for the elevators.

The door to the office said only THEO. NOVELLI & SONS, INC. I wished I had asked Carla for more information. What did they really do—any of them?

There was no receptionist at the walnut desk, which was too large for the small front office, nor was there any sign a receptionist had been there recently. The typewriter was covered and the desk was clean. The decor was impersonal—two brown tweed chairs and a small walnut table, a couple of cheap Pointillist prints, and an unhappy schefflera in an orange pot. One of the buttons on the telephone glowed, so someone was there somewhere.

I moved to the inner door and peered down the short hallway. Two closed doors, then an open one.

"Hello!" I called as I walked toward the door.

No one answered, but when I reached the door I could hear the voice on the phone. I could also smell the smoke from his cigar. It smelled like riding behind an RTD bus with the top down on the Alfa in hundred-degree August smog. My nose started to twitch. I really didn't want to go in there.

Theo Novelli had white hair and dark skin, but the resemblance to John stopped there. Theo was easily fifty pounds heavier, none of it muscle, and was sweating in his white shirt and loosened paisley tie.

"Hang on," he said, putting his hand over the receiver. "I'll come get you in a second, babe."

I wasn't sure which was worse, the smoke or the "babe."

The sterile reception area felt like a reprieve. None of my friends smoked, and to me "southern California smoker" was an oxymoron or an anachronism, something like watching an immaculate gentleman in morning coat and spats walking down the street, twirling his cane, and pausing to spit on the sidewalk.

About ten minutes later Theo leaned his bulk into the doorway, winked at me, and said, "Come on."

I followed him down the hall, three paces behind. His office didn't smell any better this time. The ashtray overflowed, the in and out baskets overflowed. The impression was of bachelor quarters. I changed my mind about evidence of his prosperity, or lack thereof.

He motioned me toward a chair. "What can I do for you?"

The question was reasonable. The look that accompanied it wasn't. I was once again glad I had worn a jumpsuit, not a dress. Less exposed flesh for Theo to contemplate. I wondered if Carla had set me up. I leaped right in, so that I wouldn't have to stay any longer than necessary. I explained that I was doing an article on the wine country and added, "I need to know what kind of situation might prompt a person to use pesticides on grapes."

The leer disappeared. "Why ask me?"

He relit his cigar, in a cloud of smoke that made him look like Puff, the Magic Iguana. I sneezed.

"Gesundheit."

"Thanks. It's a question that I couldn't bring myself to ask anyone actively involved in growing grapes for wine. Carla Novelli thought you might be the person to answer it."

"Carla?" He started to laugh, a choking, wheezing kind of laugh that made his face bright pink, and I wondered about his blood pressure. When he recovered, he said, "She's hoping I'll give you some kind of shit on John, isn't she?"

"She seemed to believe that you might."

"There's shit on John, all right, but not about the winery. The winery's his baby, his bid to become old California money. No way would he jeopardize that by doing something as dumb as using pesticides on grapes. That would be cutting the kid's throat."

"Would John have been using pesticides in an unsafe manner in connection with any of his other agricultural interests?"

Theo considered that, shrugged. "Possible. But if it's happening, it's more likely that the decision was made somewhere down the line and he doesn't know about it. He's like his neighbor, the former president—he doesn't have what you'd call a hands-on management style, and he doesn't like to be bothered with details."

"Then what kind of shit is there on John?" I blurted.

He laughed his wheezing, choking laugh again. "Not going to tell you, babe. But if you ever get real close to him, ask him how he made his first half mil. That's what gave the old man a stroke."

"Tony?"

"Yeah. Poor Italian grocer, honest as the sunrise, cursed with a son who wanted to be somebody. Hates the idea of corruption in the family."

I waited for more, although I wasn't really sure I wanted to know what John had done.

"What else, babe?" Theo asked, getting restless.

"Okay," I said resolutely. "Going back to my original question, what kind of situation would cause someone to use pesticides on grapes? Carla said something about wine futures. Would someone who had speculated heavily need to do that to save an investment?"

Theo took a puff on his cigar and blew a perfect smoke ring. He smiled at me in delight. I resisted the urge to sneeze again.

"Nah," he said, still smiling. "Speculators assume risk. But not at that level. I don't know anybody who'd buy wine futures on wine that was still grapes."

"Wine on the vine?" I asked.

"What? Yeah, right. The French used to do that, they tell me, but I never heard of anybody doing it here. People buy futures on wine in the cask, before it's bottled, but not while it's still grapes."

"So you have to be a good judge of wine to buy wine futures."

"Better than I was," he said with his wheezing laugh.

"Are wine futures traded on one of the commodity exchanges?"

"Nah, it's local and independent, California Wine Futures."

"Okay. So if a winery owner didn't want to carry the entire risk of a year's output, or maybe if he needed cash, he'd call the people at California Wine Futures, and they'd put him together with someone who would buy the wine cheap, hoping to resell it at a profit several years later?"

"Hey, that's good, babe, that's pretty close."

"So who would use pesticides?"

"You're so smart, you tell me," Theo said, shrugging and filling the air with more smoke.

"Somebody desperate."

"That's what I'd say. Somebody with no money, no prospects, and a fungus. Or somebody who didn't have a winery and was into blackmail," he added thoughtfully.

"What do you mean? You mean somebody might set that up? Pesticides on the grapes now, pay later?"

"Yeah, why not?" He seemed to like the idea.

I didn't like the idea, but I had a lousy feeling I'd better follow up on it. "Okay. Thanks for your time."

"You're welcome. Any time." The leer returned.

He insisted on walking me to the door, but I managed to leave without difficulty. Besides, I thought, remembering the self-defense instructor, I didn't look compliant. Creeping paranoia!

The smell of smoke followed me down in the elevator, clinging to my clothes, renewed each time I moved. When I reached the ground-level mall, I looked for a men's store. I was confronted by so much glass and neon that I was reminded of a House of Mirrors, where surely the Fat Lady would start laughing any moment. Which of these establishments with windows of purple, fuchsia, and chartreuse would have a pair of soft blue socks? None of them, I decided, and headed for the large department store at the far end, resolutely keeping my eyes averted as I passed shoe stores with displays of sandals, white, pink, blue, bone, green, silver, copper, low heels, high heels, wedge heels, which I was not going to buy today.

As I moved from doorway to doorway, the music changed from one loud rock selection to another, competing and then blending and then competing again. I wondered if someone more sophisticated than I in the nuances of rock could actually tell something about the store by standing in front and listening to the music. To me, they all sounded like places I didn't want to go into.

The department store was reassuringly quiet. My ears were so battered that I wouldn't have minded Muzak, but quiet was better. I found the men's department in a small corner, away from the main traffic area. The displays were dark suits with white shirts, as reassuringly conservative as the quiet, even if not very L.A. I didn't see any soft, pale blue socks. I also didn't see a clerk. I walked back out into the cacophony.

I found a store where the display was all white—tennis wear, mostly, other sports stuff, too. The music was not promising, but I entered anyway. A southern California golden boy appeared at my side, smiling, and I explained what I was looking for.

"I don't think we have blue," he said, wrinkling his charming brow in furious thought. "But let me see. Over here."

I followed him to a counter from which he produced an assortment of soft white socks.

"Will any of these do?" he asked hopefully.

I felt them carefully. Two or three of them seemed as if they might be all right, if Tony would accept white instead of blue. I bought two pair.

I was blasted by the heat when I left the mall, but it was worse when I got back to the house. The fans weren't cutting it much. I stripped the smelly clothes and started a bath.

"Cut it out," I said to Chandra, who sat there holding her paw pitifully. "Cats don't die from sprained elbows. I have to go back to Santa Clarissa tomorrow, and if you're not all well

178

when I get home, you have to go to the vet. And while I sympathize, you're not going to make me feel guilty."

Chandra just stared at me, clearly unhappy with the situation. This had to be tough on Chandra. While most cats will slink around partly opened doors, my ex-lover Mark had taught Chandra to open doors. She would sit and push with her paw, watching the door swing open, before she would march into a room. Now she couldn't even slink gracefully.

"You get better or I'm going to start calling you Chandra the Gimp."

Chandra limped off, flicking the black plume she called a tail.

Messages. John had called. He left a number for me to call in New York. A hang-up. Eva had called. Mail. Two credit card bills, a Thrifty Drug circular, and a letter from my congressman, assuring me that he was against crime, for health insurance, concerned about senior citizens, and wanted my vote.

I called Eva.

"I wanted to make sure you were all right," Eva said, her voice strained. "I heard about Georgia Peters's accident."

"The red Ford Escort?"

"Yes. And I haven't told you everything, and obviously I should. When will you be back?"

"Tomorrow. I'll be there tomorrow."

"Oh. Good. I could meet you for lunch at the Mission Inn."

"Fine, let's do that."

We hung up. I didn't want to make any more phone calls. I switched on the computer, to see if there was balm in Gilead. There wasn't. I turned it off. I decided to go for a walk and figure out what I wanted for dinner. It was too hot to think about food.

That night the heat wave broke, and the sky was overcast when I woke up Tuesday morning. Bubba was at one corner of the bed, Marcia at one, and Blaze was curled in a tight little knot against my back. They really didn't like each other much, although they all got along with Chandra. I found Chandra when I went out to pick up the paper—sitting on the roof of the house next door, paw still dangling.

"If that's your way of telling me you're better, I accept it," I called up to her.

The filtered sun made rainbow angels on a spiderweb spun between two rose bushes.

I was on the road by nine, early enough that I could see Cheverin before my late lunch with Eva.

Backed up by Santa Barbara traffic, I saw someone shinning up the traffic light pole, retrieving the doll's head. I leaned on the Ford's tinny horn.

The one advantage of the Ford over the Alfa was air conditioning. I had to roll the window down to yell.

"Russ!"

He slipped between parked cars, stopped cars, and into the passenger seat.

"Hi, Mom," he said, but his grin had somehow slipped, too.

"Tell me about it, kid."

"I found the doll's head, and it was funny when I put it up there, but it just doesn't seem funny now."

"I know the feeling. Some jokes get worse with time."

"Yeah."

"Where did you find the doll's head?"

"Chopped up, with a lot of other doll parts, when I was riding. Like the place where the dolls go to die. I don't even know why I picked it up."

"Do you want to show me?"

"Sure. My car's right around the corner. You can follow me to the ranch."

"To the ranch?"

"Yeah. I'm afraid it's too far to make it on foot. We have to ride."

The thought of spending a couple of hours on Jenny made my heart consider stopping as an alternative. Hyperventilation was right around the corner.

"Okay," I said, breathing very carefully and willing my

heart to pound normally. My jeans would be fine, and at least these sandals were old. "Where's your car?"

"Turn right here."

It took me another block to pull over, so I circled around to the yellow Mercedes. He drove off down a side street, and I discovered that there were faster ways to get through Santa Barbara.

Once we turned onto the highway, he took off, evidently assuming I knew the way. In the Alfa I could have kept up with him. In the Ford, I reached the ranch about ten minutes later. The two horses were already saddled.

I patted Jenny, and imagined the horse remembered me. In any case, mounting was not as painful as I feared it would be. Russ led the way up the same trail we had used before, but instead of turning down toward the Novelli Winery, he took me farther up the dry, brown mountain. At the foot of a live oak tree that looked as old as the Spanish conquerors, he dismounted.

I slid off Jenny, with much less grace. Imitating Russ, I pulled the reins over the horse's head and kept them in my hand.

"There," he said, pointing.

Someone had violently dismembered a collection of perhaps a dozen dolls. Heads, torsos, arms, legs, all piled grotesquely. Painted blue glass eyes stared at me. Red mouths smiled. Blond wigs, brown wigs were strewn loosely around. Little pink and white ruffles, torn from little pink and white dresses, were ground into the dirt.

"When did you find this?" I asked.

"A few weeks ago. I'm not sure. I think it was maybe a week before the guy died in the wine cellar."

"Do you have any idea whose dolls they were, who might have done this?"

"You gotta be kidding."

"Right." I stared a moment longer, at the dolls that lost the battle. Did it matter who won? What did this have to do with anything?

I became increasingly uncomfortable. Someone had gone crazy, someone had destroyed a child's dreams.

"Let's leave," I said.

We rode back to the ranch in silence.

"What do you think?" Russ asked as we reached the barn.

"I think I don't know very much," I answered. "I think I don't understand much of anything. I also think I need to get to the Mission Inn or I'll be late to meet Eva for lunch."

"Eva?"

"Yes. Eva Novelli. She called yesterday, and I said I'd meet her for lunch. What's wrong?"

"I guess because of Will—I just didn't know you were her friend."

"Friend is probably too strong a word, although I do like her. That doesn't mean I didn't like Will. I'm not in a position where I have to take sides—or at least I don't feel that I do. I also feel I don't have enough information, and that the whole thing took place a long time ago."

"Will remembered. I want you to know, he felt bad about what happened, and Eva would never listen to him. Eva called him a lot of names, you know, or he never would have hit her."

"I'm sure he felt bad." I believed Eva hadn't listened. I believed Eva had called Will names. And I believed Will regretted hitting her. I reached out and touched Russ's cheek. "I gotta go, kid. Take care of yourself, and stay in touch. Wait a minute." I had locked my things in the trunk of the car, keeping only the keys with me on the ride. I retrieved my purse from the car, pulled out one of my business cards, and handed it to him. "I want you to be able to stay in touch. Call me in L.A. if you want to."

"Okay, I will. Thanks."

I knew I should have spent more time with Russ, but I needed to find out what Eva had to tell me. And the dolls had upset me. I needed to process the broken bodies of the dolls. I would have to do something about Russ later, somehow.

When I arrived at the Mission Inn, there was a message

182

from Eva saying that she would be unable to make lunch but would call the hotel later. I booked a room, figuring that meant I'd be staying the night. It would have been too late to drive back after dinner with Tom anyway. Besides, I needed to get rid of Jenny's smell before seeing anyone else.

That done, I ate a quick sandwich in the coffee shop and drove to the garage in Los Robles.

"Maybe early next week," was all the man would say. On the subject of sabotage, he was firmly noncommittal.

I was starting to fret over the visibility of the red Ford Escort—not that the Alfa would be any less noticeable—but at least it was faster, and I wished that I had changed cars in Santa Barbara. I might do that this afternoon.

I passed Polarity on my way to the Lindale Winery and decided to stop on the way back.

When I reached the Lindale Winery, one of the college kids pointed me out toward one of the fields. I could make out a man, apparently with some kind of portable equipment, and was glad I had finally learned my lesson about the kind of shoes to wear around wineries. The man was Henri Cheverin, and in answer to my question he explained that he was testing the acid content of the grapes. A tall man, with a long, weathered face, gray-haired, dressed in gray work shirt and pants, he examined my face with intent black eyes as I introduced myself and told him what I knew of his background (minus John's cold stare when I said I was going to talk with him). I began to feel uncomfortable, and imagined his grapes feeling the same way under the intense gaze.

"What do you want to know?"

"I'd like to know something more about you. For example, why did you leave Novelli?"

"There's nothing mysterious about it. Lindale is bigger, offered a greater challenge, more responsibility." He paused. "And Lindale himself is an honorable man."

"Are you saying that Novelli isn't?"

The intent gaze didn't waver. "I'm only saying that Lindale is."

"Could you tell me what happened between you and John Novelli?"

"I told you. Nothing."

I almost believed him.

"What about your work at the Cahill Winery? Isn't it difficult to handle an operation this big and still have time to supervise that one as well?"

The eyes flickered and looked away, back to his test tubes.

"I make time. Alida is a very special woman, and—she needs a good winemaker. And sometimes one can do very interesting experiments at a small winery, ones that would not be considered worthwhile at a large one. It is worth the time I spend."

Of course. One more piece of the puzzle. Henri Cheverin was in love with Alida Cahill. And she needed him. No wonder he had left the Novelli Winery, and she denied ever having been involved with John.

"I've heard a rumor that some winery in the valley has contaminated wine on the market—would you know anything about that?"

He snapped around with fury boiling in the depth of his eyes. His voice was calm.

"No one in this valley would use pesticides on grapes."

John Novelli's voice echoed in my head.

"But perhaps someone in this valley unknowingly bought grapes tainted with pesticides. Isn't that possible?"

The fury boiled over into his mouth, erupted like Mount St. Helens. "What do you want me to say to you? Rick Clarence was an evil man. He deserved to die. Now get out of here."

"But why did he deserve to die?" I cried desperately. "And who killed him?"

"Poison," he shouted. "Poison! Not the poison in the grapes—the poison in the valley! Who is the poison in the valley?"

He stared at me, reminding me of John the Baptist, the voice crying in the wilderness. And then he calmed, drew himself erect.

"Please leave now," he said quietly. "Please leave. I have work to do."

I backed away, embarrassed. Perhaps dear Theo had something in his theory about planted pesticides. And Henri knew. It seemed unlikely that the grapes were sold to Lindale, not with the extent of their vineyard. But Cahill? Blackmailing Alida seemed far more likely—and gave Henri a motive for murder.

I returned to Polarity, certain that Cindy Frawn would soothe my distraught soul.

"What I need to know," I said, cup of herb tea in hand, "is who might be financially unable to handle recalling a year's output, if there was something wrong with the wine. I know this means you have to violate a confidence, but it may help us find out who killed Rick." I winced at what I was leaving out. I felt cold. "Is there anybody so close to the edge that one bad season would have wiped them out?"

"I don't do everybody's books, of course," Cindy replied, uncertainly. "I don't do any of the bigger ones, like Lindale, and I told you that Francesca Novelli does her own."

"I know. But the bigger wineries are likely to have sources of credit, and they could probably pull one year off the market without anyone really noticing. Particularly one like Lindale, trying to make a name. Just say it isn't up to their standard. And Novelli—well, let's skip them for the moment. Maybe they could do that, too. What about the others?"

Cindy sat there, looking down at her herb tea. Tessa trotted over, concerned, and Cindy put the tea down to hug the dog for a moment.

"When Alida Cahill got a divorce three years ago, she got the winery, but not a lot of cash. The rumor was that she thought she wouldn't need it, she thought John Novelli would marry her. He didn't, of course, and she had to borrow a lot to stay in business. If she'd lost a season, she would probably have lost the winery as well."

"Okay. Anybody else?"

Cindy shook her head. "Nobody I know of. I just can't imagine Alida killing anybody, though. I really can't."

"Yeah, I know. I know how you feel. And probably she didn't." But Henri Cheverin is a scientist, comfortable with test tubes, loving Alida, hating John. What better revenge than to murder Rick—who was blackmailing Alida—and leave the body in John's wine cellar?

"I need to know something else," I continued. "It appears to me that just about everyone around here grows their own grapes. Does anyone buy grapes? Or has anyone bought grapes?"

"Sometimes, sure, some people do. We never have. The year of the divorce, though, everything went bad for Alida. Including the grapes. Part of her cash flow problem was that she had to buy grapes."

"Anybody else?"

"Oh God, this looks bad for Alida, I know, and I just don't believe she did it. Maybe I should call her."

"Cindy, please, I'm not sure that's a good idea. I'll tell you what. I'll talk to her, and I'll let you know what she says. Okay?"

"Would you?" Cindy brightened immediately. She obviously wanted out of that chore. "That would be wonderful."

"I would. And I'm sure it'll be all right." Sort of sure. Henri Cheverin was now fighting with Michael Garth for number-one suspect. Even if all the pieces didn't quite fit.

First things first, I thought as I drove away from Polarity. Get rid of this car. Exchange it for a brown one, nobody notices brown cars.

I had to pass the Novelli Winery on the way out of Santa Clarissa, and I turned in. There were several cars in the parking lot, and I parked mine among them and walked across the lawn to the house. Tony was on his patio, sitting quietly. I accepted his offer of a Perrier.

"I looked for blue," I said, pulling the bag with the socks out of my purse, "but white was all I could find in soft socks. Is white okay, or do you want me to dye them?"

Tony fumbled in the bag with his good hand, then focused on the socks, feeling them carefully.

"Fine," he whispered. "They're fine. Thanks."

"You're welcome."

Silence. Tony seemed comfortable with silence. I wasn't. I sat there watching shadows creep across the lawn, pondering whether I was more uncomfortable with silence or with asking questions about the murder. On my last trip, I had thought about taking Tony out someplace, to a movie, on a picnic, but now I felt too spiritless to ask him. And too frightened. All my time and energies would have to go toward finding out what happened, at least for the moment.

"Tony, I need to find out who killed Rick Clarence."

"What?"

I repeated the question. Tony waved his arm vaguely and then dropped it, without saying anything.

"I thought maybe, because you're here all the time, maybe you saw something that night, or heard something, maybe you might know who was here."

"Will asked that," he said, nodding.

"What did you tell him?"

"People. There were people here."

"Was John here?"

"People," Tony continued firmly. "Voices. I don't know who."

"Men? Women?"

"Both."

"Could you tell how many?"

"No." Tony's mouth was working oddly. He rang his bell. "I have to go in now," he said, as Lucy appeared.

"Okay," I sighed. "Okay. I hope I see you soon."

"Bye," Tony said, waving.

"Bye-bye," Lucy said, cheerfully.

"Bye."

Whatever Tony knew, he wasn't going to tell me. But if Tony knew something, surely Francesca must know it, too. Would Francesca talk to me? Not likely, but I'd try. And maybe Francesca would talk to Eva, maybe I could ask Eva for help with Francesca.

Francesca was just bringing a tour group into the tasting room. I watched as she and Diane handed out glasses to the half-dozen couples, waited until the crowd was wandering among the T-shirts and mustard, and then asked Francesca if she had a moment.

"I'm afraid not," Francesca said with something more than her usual cool.

"Francesca, it's important. I need to know who was here the night Rick Clarence died, I need to know who's trying to kill me. Please."

Francesca wavered for a minute. "I don't know what you're talking about. There wasn't anybody here that night, as far as I know."

"Tony said he heard voices."

"Tony's half deaf. If he heard voices, they were in his head."

"Somebody had to be here. Rick Clarence was here, and the person who murdered him." My voice was strident.

Diane stared at the two of us in horror. "The tourists," she hissed.

"Who was it?" I whispered.

"I don't know," Francesca said fiercely, as she turned to a young couple in jeans and smiled. "This next wine is a Chenin Blanc."

I felt like an idiot, standing there, so I left.

I exchanged cars in Santa Barbara. I didn't like the brown Honda any more than I had liked the red Ford, but at least I felt less conspicuous.

Once more at the Mission Inn, I called the number in New York that John had left.

"Where are you?" he exploded.

I told him as much as I wanted him to know, which wasn't much.

"I'll be back Thursday. In the meantime, I think you should stay at the house. You'll be safe there."

"With Francesca and Tony and Lucy? I'm just as safe at the hotel."

"Derek's there. And I want you protected. I'll call and let them know."

"No. I don't want to stay there. And nobody but Tony would want me to. And I'm not as certain about him, after this afternoon."

"You're reading too much into that. He has trouble with his bladder, and he probably didn't want to tell you that he needed to relieve himself. And Francesca's right—he's half deaf and couldn't have heard anything, even if there was something to hear."

I thought about that. "I'm still staying at the hotel. Call me when you get back. I'll be either here or at home." I paused again. "I do want to see you."

"I want to see you, too." Softer. His voice was gentle again. "We'll talk more when I'm back."

I tried to get Eva, but the machine answered at the office, and there was no answer at the ranch. I would try again in the morning. It was time to meet Tom.

He was waiting for me at the restaurant in the Los Robles Hotel, at a table in back, staring out the window at the brown hills. He didn't see me, and I tried to assess him as I would if I were meeting him for the first time. There was no way around it. He was as handsome as any ex-Marine, ex-cop, dropout writer who had let his hair grow could possibly be. And I cared about him. But not enough.

I stared until he turned, jumped to his feet to wave me over. I offered my cheek when he leaned down to kiss me.

"Shit," he said. "Is it because of that smooth son of a bitch Novelli?"

"No, it isn't," I answered honestly. "I told you before. It's because of me."

Maybe the evening wasn't quite as bad as walking barefoot through a Georgia swamp. But maybe it was a toss-up. It even had its good moments, although I couldn't remember any of them later. I only remembered how he flared after he pushed me into disclosing that I had some ideas about Rick Clarence's murder.

"God damn it! I thought I told you to leave that to the professionals!"

"You did. But one of the professionals is dead," I said, seething. "And the other one isn't very professional. If these murders—and it isn't just Rick Clarence anymore—are going to be solved, somebody has to care enough to do something. Somebody has to take a stand."

He looked at me as intently as Henri Cheverin had.

"Is that what you think this is about—caring enough to take a stand? Is that what you think murder is about? Is that why you think I left the force—because I didn't care enough to take a stand?"

I couldn't meet his eyes. And I couldn't tell him I was in it because I thought somebody was after me. I just wanted out of the relationship.

"No. No, I don't think that. I really don't. But my decisions aren't based on you, on what you chose about your life, even though I respect that." I looked back at him. "I'm in this—involved in this, with these people—and I am going to see it through."

"I guess you're on your own, lady," was all he said.

I felt a small twinge, watching him walk out. But not much.

13

"What are you accusing me of?" Alida demanded.

Alida was the only person in the tasting room, again. I wondered if there was ever much traffic. A small winery in the middle of nowhere seemed like a tough way to go it alone.

"I'm not accusing you of anything. I'm wondering if maybe Rick was blackmailing you, and if you saw him that night, that's all."

"And if I killed him?"

"I have trouble with that. If I really thought you killed him, I wouldn't be talking to you about it. Because that would mean that you also tried to kill me. But I'm trying to put together what happened that night, and I'm interested in whether you had a motive—like getting rid of a blackmailer. Do you?"

Alida barked a short laugh. "Why would I answer that? You're not the police."

"Well, I thought that's why you might. I haven't talked to

the police—not that I could count on Jerry Harris to be effective even if I had—and I thought maybe you'd rather talk to me. For one thing, I'm likely to be a lot more sympathetic about Rick blackmailing you—if he was. For another, you might be able to shed some light on who else might have a motive. And I know he saw you the night he was murdered, or at least he planned to—it was in his calendar." Good detectives take wild guesses. Sometimes they even lie.

Alida appraised me. "With the right equipment, you know, a person can uncork and recork—even reseal—a bottle of wine, and it would take an FDA inspection to prove it had ever been tampered with."

"And?"

"Rick said he had proof that there were residual pesticides in the '88 white Zinfandel. We didn't grow all of those grapes, we bought them, so I suppose it's possible that he was telling the truth. I couldn't afford to have him make the accusation public."

"But you think he faked his test?"

"Yes, of course. Who would use pesticides on grapes? And I think he would have faked another one, and even if I managed to get other testers to say that there were no pesticides in the wine, which I would, the story would be hard to kill. For years, people would be saying, 'Cahill Winery—wasn't that the one with the pesticide scandal?' That's all anyone would remember."

If my theory was right, the test wasn't what Rick set up. And other testers would have corroborated the results.

"So he was blackmailing you?"

"Yes."

"What did he want to back off?"

"Half the winery."

"He wanted you to give him half the winery?"

"That's it."

"Why? I'm sorry, but it doesn't seem that profitable. Why did he want it?"

"He wanted to start making wine. He had some ideas he

wanted to test. And it was easier to walk into a going operation than raise the money to set one up. And I think he was a mean, devious human being, and setting up this plot amused him."

"And you said no."

"I told him I'd have to think about it. I told him I'd meet him here, and we could talk. He didn't show up. I found out later he was dead, and I have to say I was glad."

Alida's voice had been steady as she spoke, her eyes unblinking. I was certain that part of the story was true, certain that Alida was glad he was dead, not quite so certain that she didn't know more about it.

"You were going to meet him here—not at the Novelli Winery?"

"Why would I meet him there?"

"I don't know, but that's where he was. Why was *he* there?"

"Meeting someone else? Blackmailing someone else?" Alida shrugged.

"Who could he be blackmailing at Novelli? John?"

"Not John," Alida said, with a small laugh. "Surely you know him well enough to know that John would not be blackmailed."

"Do you really think John would have murdered someone first?"

"There is no doubt in my mind."

"Maybe you attract men capable of murder. What about Henri Cheverin?"

Alida blinked.

"Henri? Capable of murder?"

"Why not? You're being blackmailed, he's in love with you, he decides to save you, why not?"

Alida bleated. It was a funny little laugh that I could only think of as a bleat.

"Well, because he was here that night. If you're looking for alibis, he has one. I don't know if that will mean anything to you, that we were together. I suppose you're capable of thinking up some kind of conspiracy theory, that Henri and I were in this together, but the simple truth is that I didn't want to meet Rick alone. Henri was here, and he stayed, although I don't know why that's any of your business, and I frankly dislike you, and I wish you would leave."

Alida stared uncompromisingly at me, and I realized I wasn't going to learn anything more, not now. This sounded like the truth, and I hoped it was. I wanted to ask where Russ was, but I didn't think that would endear me to Alida, who would probably misinterpret my interest.

I stopped to scratch the ears of the ginger cat on my way out. I liked that fat ginger cat better than anything else about Alida. That wasn't fair. I liked Russ, even better than the cat.

Well, I had certainly tied Alida to Rick Clarence. And Henri Cheverin. And had an update for my Suspects file.

I still had time to catch Michael Garth before my re-scheduled lunch with Eva. Part of me knew it was dumb, wandering around up here asking people if they had killed Rick Clarence, and if not, if they knew who had, knowing one of them might try again to kill me. But whenever I thought about what else I might be doing, I came up blank. I simply didn't know what else to do but walk in and ask Michael if he had killed Rick Clarence.

"Where do you get off?" Michael screamed. "What makes you think I even knew him?"

"Whether you knew him or not, I think you knew about him. I think you knew he had messed Phil's life up once, and now he wanted to come back. And that would mess your life up as well. You would have known where the key to the Novelli wine cellar was. You might even have had Phil's key. You arranged to meet him at the Novelli Winery so that suspicion would fall there, not here. And Phil was safe because he was out of town. You had doctored and resealed a bottle of wine—say, the 1987 Pinot Noir Reserve—and you suggested that the two of you have a glass of wine and talk it over. But you didn't drink. He did. You left him there dead and came back here."

194

"What the hell kind of evidence do you have?"

"Someone heard shouting. And Rick Clarence wrote every-thing down in his calendar." How was that for evading the question?

"Would I have been shouting at him if I were going to kill him? Would I have been shouting at him while I was trying to get him to drink a carefully prepared bottle of poisoned wine? Think it through, lady. And you haven't seen any calen-dar."

"There you're wrong. I did see the calendar."

"But you didn't get any evidence out of it. I talked to Baca. The pages were missing."

"You talked to Will?" I said, off guard.

"Yes, I did." Michael was red-faced, spitting the words. "He thought I did it, too. And I told him that I met Clarence at the Novelli Winery—at his suggestion, not mine—and that I left him alive. He had a later date."

"What did Rick Clarence want with you?"

"Everything I had—he wanted Phil and the winery. And he said he'd destroy us if I didn't leave."

"He'd say that there were traces of pesticides in your wine."

"Exactly."

One winery or another, Clarence would end up with some-thing.

"Did Will believe you?"

"He didn't arrest me, did he?"

"No, but maybe he didn't have time."

Michael took that in. "He wasn't going to arrest me. He was going to see if Clarence had tried to blackmail anybody else."

"Do you know of anyone else?"

"I wouldn't tell you if I did. I hope whoever killed him gets away with it."

Michael made it clear that I was dismissed.

When I reached the Mission Inn, Eva was waiting, clearly tired, pale blue smudges in the thin skin under her eyes making her look ten years older. There was something waif-like about her, her competence giving way to vulnerability, and I wanted to hold her.

But when I reached for her, Eva shrank back and turned toward the dining room as if she hadn't seen the gesture.

Eva ordered a bowl of gazpacho without looking at the menu. I was losing my appetite, watching those strained eyes, eyes that didn't want to meet mine. I ordered gazpacho and iced tea, feeling once more that it was easier to let Eva make the decisions about food—something that would have bothered me if she'd been a man.

"Well?" I prompted, when the waiter had left and Eva still stared out the window.

"This is probably a mistake, but I don't know what else to do."

She was silent again. I sat through the silence, waited it out.

"Something's wrong with Francesca. I think I've known that for a while, and I haven't really wanted to face it. She's been leaving messages on my answering machine, late at night when she's knows I'm not there, long messages, about love and hate and avenging angels, about the destruction of the dolls, about Papa. I think she may have done something she doesn't want him to know about. When I ask her about the messages, she pretends ignorance. But I know it's her voice, and she's the only one who would leave those messages."

It sounded strange, Eva calling John "Papa."

"The destruction of the dolls? Does Francesca have a doll collection?"

"Yes."

"What did it mean to her?"

"Francesca and I had very different relationships with our father. He had wanted me for his partner—his winemaker—and he always treated me as an equal. Francesca was his baby, his little girl friend. Whenever he came back from a business trip, he bought her a doll. Mexican dolls, French dolls, whatever. And he would tell her stories about the dolls.

196

So the destruction of the dolls would be the destruction of their relationship. I think she's trying to tell me that something has destroyed their relationship, and she has to avenge it."

"Why are you telling me now?"

"I thought, since you're up here asking questions, maybe you could find out, somehow, what she's done."

"Do you think it has something to do with the rest of what's going on?" I didn't want to say "murder."

"I don't know. I only thought—I'm afraid—it's happening at the same time, you know."

"Have you talked to anyone else about it? What about the authorities?"

"What authorities? Who? I'm telling you because I need to tell someone, and because maybe you can find something out. And because I want you to come to me with whatever it is. If she really has done something, I want her helped and protected, not persecuted, not caught by an unfeeling male-dominated system."

"I don't know what I can do. She surely won't talk to me. I'll have to try something else. As a matter of fact, I was hoping she would talk to you."

The gazpacho arrived, bright red with things floating in it. I wished I hadn't ordered gazpacho. I buttered a piece of bread.

"I'll have to think about it," I continued. "And I thought you told me she didn't know Rick Clarence."

"She didn't, as far as I know. But she certainly knew of him. And perhaps he got in touch with her."

"You knew he was blackmailing wineries?"

"I heard a rumor. Michael Garth said more than he intended one drunken afternoon."

"Why didn't you tell me?"

Eva shrugged, smiled wryly. "I didn't tell you everything."

"Anything else I ought to know?"

"If I think of anything, I'll call you."

Eva couldn't finish her gazpacho either.

What to do, I mused, back in the cool, shadowed room after lunch. My only plan seemed dumb. But it was my only plan. I walked to the hardware store, walked back to the hotel.

All I could manage to do for the rest of the afternoon was stare out the window of the room. I couldn't read, I certainly couldn't nap. When it turned dark outside, I went downstairs to the dining room. I knew I should eat, but I still couldn't manage to deal with food. I had one cappuccino, then moved to the bar.

I sat there drinking coffee and nursing a single brandy, alone except for a bartender who clearly resented my presence, until it closed at two in the morning. Not that I was afraid of falling asleep. But sitting in the bar was a way of killing time until it was late enough to go.

The brown Honda was the only car on the road. When I reached the turnoff to the Novelli Winery, I pulled over, parked and locked the car, taking only my keys and my recently purchased flashlight. My sneakers crunched softly in the gravel as I walked down the drive. The moon was full, and the stars showered me with so much light that I could see easily. I hoped no one was around to see me. My heart was beating so hard that I could feel the pulse in my ears. Don't hyperventilate, I thought, wishing I hadn't drunk so much coffee, wishing again that I hadn't given up Valium, wishing I hadn't decided to do this.

The black Cadillac was parked in front of the house. I knew John wasn't there, but Derek must be. Damn. I hoped he was a sound sleeper.

I moved onto the grass and started around the house. Why hadn't I come up behind the house, where there were trees and shadows? At least there were no dogs to worry about.

Shadows, now. I sat down and leaned against a tree, willing my heart to slow down. Make your mind like a clear blue lake, I chanted silently, forcing myself to breathe deeply and evenly. The pulse slowed, the mind calmed, I got up and headed toward the patio off John's bedroom.

When my feet touched stone I paused, making sure I knew

where the furniture was, thinking this was not the moment to bump into anything, glad I could still amuse myself with visions of clumsiness. Placing my feet carefully, I almost glided to the sliding door. The screen wasn't locked, but it wasn't going to slide quietly. I moved it an inch, wanting to check the glass door before going farther. It stood firm, locked from the inside. Someone good at this kind of thing could probably get in easily. A male friend had once lifted a door like this out of its groove, to show me how easy it was. I decided to check the bathroom window before I tried lifting doors.

The bathroom screen was hooked shut, but the stained-glass window with the lilies of the valley was open. I used my keys to poke a hole in the bottom of the screen so that I could reach the hook, scraping my fingers in the process. Something was still holding the screen. Feeling carefully up the sides, I found a large nail on each side and used my keys to pry them up. The screen swung loose from its top hooks. I lifted it off and laid it against the side of the house.

I tucked my keys in my back pocket and tucked the flash-light inside my sweatshirt, using the band of my bra to hold it in place. With both hands firmly on the sill I jumped up, leaning so that my hips were against the window ledge, catching my toes against the wall, pulling up one knee and pushing through. I paused for a moment to suck my scraped fingers.

The moonlight barely reached the bathroom. Although this was probably as safe as anywhere to use the flashlight, I didn't turn it on. Cat's eyes. Think of cat's eyes. Use all the available light. I could see outlines. And I had been there before, I knew where the tub, the shower, the toilet, the basin were.

Tile, rug, tile underfoot. The door to the bedroom in front of me, the doorjamb in my hand. The drapes were closed, and no light reached the bedroom, not even for my cat's eyes. I pointed the flashlight toward the floor as I switched it on, moved the beam carefully around the room, keeping it low. For a fleeting moment I wished that I would find John in the big bed, that I could crawl in beside him, waking him slowly with my body, not explaining my presence. And forget about this nonsense, finding things out that I didn't really want to know.

The bed. I crept around the bed, shoulders hunched, not allowing myself to stop. The office door in front of me. The door handle was cold. It turned quietly, the door making no noise. The door leading to the rest of the house was open, and I quickly switched the flashlight off. I leaned against the wall, remembering the office, John's desk, the desk with the computer. If I walked straight ahead, I should reach the door without stumbling.

My hand touched the door, swung it shut. I had to risk the flashlight again, to turn the computer on. Damn! The fan! More risk. But surely, surely, it was only inside this closed office that the computer's fan sounded like an airplane engine.

The machine tested itself, all 640K. And then something appeared on the screen. I began to chuckle, but stifled the sound. I had forgotten to bring my glasses, and whatever the computer wanted to tell me was going to be a bitch to read. I played with brightness and contrast, manipulating the controls until the light from the amber letters on the screen lent a faint illumination to the keyboard. By leaning back and tilting my head slightly to one side I could focus well enough to make out the words.

The machine wanted a password. I had been congratulating myself on my luck—the machine had a hard disk, no floppies to sort through until dawn, hoping to find the right one—and now the machine wanted a password.

Best to start with obvious ones, hoping that the computer didn't set off an alarm after three wrong guesses. I tried John, Francesca, Books, Wine, Eva, Carla, Tony, Dolls, Papa.

"Try Grapes," said a soft voice behind me.

I squeaked. I had wanted to scream, but my throat closed, and it came out a squeak. My hands froze on the keyboard. I was afraid to turn around, knowing that whoever it was could see me in the computer's glow, but I would be blind.

200

"Why don't I just turn it off?" I had no air in my lungs and could barely get the words out. Breathe, I thought, but my lungs didn't want to respond.

"Not yet. Try Grapes."

My fingers weren't responding any better than my lungs. It took me three tries to type Grapes and hit ENTER. The screen filled with words and numbers, all blurry.

"There it is."

"Look, I don't have my glasses, I can't see any of this anyway, so I'll exit from the program and turn it off." My voice was coming back, but it still wasn't strong.

"It probably wouldn't mean much to you anyway. It's the financial history of the winery, including a record of grape purchases over the years."

"There really were pesticides in the wine one year."

"Yes. But Clarence didn't need his spectrometer to prove it. He was part owner of the vineyard that Cahill and Novelli both bought grapes from. He set us up."

"And so you killed him?"

Soft laugh. "No, I didn't kill him. She did. If she had told me in advance what she was going to do, I would have stopped her. If she hadn't panicked, I could have gotten rid of the body. But then I had to protect her."

"So you killed Will Baca. And you overheard my conversations with John, so you knew I was asking questions, and you tried to kill me."

"Yes."

"Didn't she care?"

"Will took Eva away, and he hurt her. I thought about killing him a long time ago. I wanted to. And we talked about you. She said you were dangerous, and she's right. You could make us very unhappy."

If I could kill the computer screen, maybe I could get away in the dark. I began edging my hand toward the switch.

"Why did she kill Clarence herself? Why not turn him over to you or her father?"

"For her, it was worse than the threat about the wine. She

made a mistake. Her father trusted her to run the winery, needed her to run the winery, and she made a mistake. In a year when we needed more grapes, she bought them from the wrong person, because he said he knew Eva, knew Phil. She trusted him. Too much. She even thought she loved him. Then she made another mistake. She gave him money, thinking he would leave her alone. He wouldn't, of course. I could have told her that. She didn't tell me about it, didn't tell me when she decided not to give him any more. But then he threatened to tell her father, make a fool of her before her father. Blame the purchase of the tainted grapes, then the cover-up, on her. Her father is very important to her, you know. He's so proud of her, he's left all the business of the winery to her, and she didn't want him to be ashamed."

Of course. That was what I kept forgetting. John didn't take care of the winery business. Francesca did.

"He's proud of the winery, too," the voice continued, "and she didn't want him ever to know about the grapes. And I think she really wanted to do it herself. There was something in her that enjoyed it, the way John would have twenty years ago." There was a pause. Some kind of movement. "Clarence said there were pesticides in the wine. He was right. He set it up, a long time ago, and waited patiently. He waited until the wines were out of the barrels, until they were bottled and sold. Then he made his move. And she stopped him."

I knew that was the end of the speech. Which door should I head for? The bedroom, back out the window, I'd never make it through the house. In one motion I turned off the computer and lunged for the door, hoping and fearing that I had destroyed the records. But the room was suddenly bright, blinding me, paralyzing me. Derek stood across the room, fully dressed in his black chauffeur's uniform, his hand on the light switch.

He smiled at me. I had never seen him smile before, never seen any expression on his doggy face but obedience. It was grotesque, like the smiles on the dead dolls.

"The bedroom," he said. "That's a good idea. You've been there before, after all."

"So have a lot of others," I blurted.

"Not here. You're the only one he brought here. He shouldn't have done that. It upset her, a lot. I think she might like seeing you there dead."

He started toward me, still smiling.

I would have to stop him. Breathe, I thought. I couldn't stay terrified. I would not be compliant.

If you have a weapon of opportunity, use it, the self-defense instructor called out to me. I backed away from him, edging toward the desk.

"I said the bedroom," he told me softly, placing his heavy hands on my shoulders.

"No!" I shouted, bringing the flashlight down on his nose with all my strength.

I felt something give, heard the crunch. Blood spurted onto my face and chest. Something in me wanted to whimper.

"No!" I shouted again.

I turned sideways, raised my foot, and kicked down against his shin, missing his kneecap, but with enough force that he was briefly startled, long enough for me to knock the hands from my shoulders and head for the door to the living room.

I had taken two steps when I saw the gun in Francesca's hand. Derek whirled me around and slapped me so hard that I almost blacked out.

"That's enough," Francesca said sharply.

"She broke my nose," Derek whined, breathing through his mouth.

"I can see that. If you want it reset, I'll pay for it. But I don't want anything more happening in the house. We have to get her out of here."

I felt an urge to laugh, thinking of how flat Derek's nose had been even before I hit it. The choked giggle that came out sounded so much like the beginning of hysteria that it sobered me. I leaned against the wall, still dizzy.

"What do you want me to do with her? Drive her into a tree?"

Derek had wiped his face with his sleeve. I became aware of the blood again, and wiped my own face with my sleeve. I stared at the bloody sleeve.

"No more auto accidents. I think she may decide to go for a late night swim in Lake Cachuma. It's been so hot, she couldn't sleep. She ignored the NO SWIMMING sign. And poor swimmers shouldn't swim alone."

"I'm not a poor swimmer," I lied.

"You will be after Derek knocks you out," Francesca told me calmly. She moved out of the doorway. "You go first."

I didn't move. Francesca turned, following my gaze. Tony sat there, his wheelchair blocking the exit.

"Hi," he said hoarsely, as the wheelchair carried him into the room.

"Hi, Tony," I said, my eyes starting to fill.

"You can't hurt her. She's my guest," he whispered to Francesca. He held his hand out for the gun.

"No!" Francesca wailed. "No, Grandpa, you don't understand! You don't know what I've done! Papa doesn't know what I've done! I have to get rid of her!"

"I know," he said. "I know. It has to end now."

"But when Papa—Papa won't love me!"

"I'll take care of it. You can't hurt her. She's my guest."

I had seen flashes of Tony's former power. Now he had it all back. His voice was firm, his hand steady. Francesca wavered. Then she started to sob, deep, wracking sobs, the sobs of a child whose dreams are dead.

"Papa won't love me," she sobbed.

She gave him the gun and crumpled next to the wheelchair, her head in his lap.

Tony turned to me, smiling sadly.

"Please leave now."

I wanted to stay, talk to him, find a way to make everything all right, tell him that I would take him dancing.

"Goodbye, Tony. Thank you," I said. I kissed him swiftly on the top of the head as I passed.

"Bye," he whispered.

I was almost to the car when I heard the three gunshots.

14

"The worst thing, of course, was that it wasn't over," I said, refilling Elly's champagne glass. "I had to call Eva the next morning, and drive back to Santa Barbara to tell her everything Lucy didn't know. Santa Barbara was as far as I would go."

"Drive back? Where did you go?"

"I came home. I went to the hotel, grabbed my things and drove home. I couldn't stand the thought of waking up in Santa Clarissa. I wouldn't have gone to the hotel, except I couldn't stand the thought of going back to Santa Clarissa, either. I ran out of my hotel room, clothes over my arm like a madwoman. The way I drove the Honda I was lucky I *didn't* end up in Lake Cachuma."

I stuck the bottle in the ice bucket and leaned back in my chair. The coals would be ready in a minute, and I would have to do something with the turkey steaks that were marinating in red wine and olive oil and fresh thyme, but I didn't want to move yet. A slight breeze had come up in the late after-noon, and the yard was peacefully cool. Blaze was sleeping under a rose bush, Bubba and Chandra drowsing in the daisies. Marcia was nowhere to be seen, but would no doubt be heard from when she smelled turkey. Salome was trampling what was left of the strawberry plants. Looking at Salome, I almost felt guilty about the turkey steaks.

"I understand the hyperbole," Elly said thoughtfully, "but telling Eva couldn't have been worse than being threatened at gunpoint. Seriously, if you had to live through one of those moments again—"

"Stop. You win. But I felt so bad, telling her what hap-pened, that she felt she ought to comfort me. And I was truly ashamed of that. And I kept thinking there was something I could have done, so that they all didn't end up dead."

"You think you were responsible?"

"No, I can't think that, or I'd go crazy. They did it. They murdered. They were responsible. Except Tony, and I know he did what he believed he had to do. But I got involved in a stupid, awful way. Maybe Tom was right. Maybe it would have been better if I hadn't. Someone else would have found out about Francesca, surely."

"How did John take it?"

"I don't really know. He sent my manuscript back with a very polite note saying he was sorry we wouldn't have a chance to discuss it, but that he didn't feel he could see me, for a while at least. But I think it's never. I don't think we can ever face each other again. I sent his books on wine back with a similar note. And I told Fred that someone else would have to write the article. Eva and Johnny moved into the house, by the way. At least temporarily. She didn't want John be alone."

We sat in silence broken abruptly by salsa music blasting from the house beyond the backyard fence. Someone must have realized it was too loud, because it was turned down almost immediately. We could still hear it, though. I hate salsa music.

"Time for the turkey steaks," I said.

I set the table with the cold eggplant salad, the marinated green beans, the warm sourdough rolls, and the strawberries soaked in Grand Marnier that were really for dessert, but I didn't want to go back in the house for them. The turkey didn't take long.

We talked very little during dinner. I fed bits of turkey to Bubba, Chandra, and Blaze. Elly fed bits of turkey to Marcia. Elly liked Marcia, and I kept hoping she would take her.

"What are you going to do now?" Elly finally asked, when the table was cleared, and we sat by candlelight with the last of a second bottle of champagne, watching Chandra groom the turkey scraps off Bubba's face.

I shrugged. "My book, I guess. I told Fred I wanted a little time off. I need to work on something else, where I don't have to ask any questions."

"That's not quite what I meant. You really shouldn't be alone either, you know, and I have to leave."

"I'm not alone. I have four cats and Salome. There's always a lot going on here. It's really not the same as living alone."

"You could call Tom."

"I wish you'd stop that. You sound like my mother, wanting me to be married off before it's too late, when it's already too late, and probably was when I was nineteen. I'm frankly happier with the cats. They're less demanding than a man, and they love me without qualification. Cats still love you when you're crying and you smell bad."

"Sometimes people do, too."

"I know." I wasn't sure I believed it. "Anyway, I'll be fine. I promise."

Elly peered at me, small eyes focusing through thick glasses. She finally nodded.

After Elly left, I stayed outside and watched the coals die. It seemed so early to go in and go to bed. And I really thought about it, but there was no one I wanted to call.

Blaze was waiting for me on the bed, dancing around with joy because I was there. Bubba jumped up, too, and Blaze screamed a Siamese war cry and hit him. He wanted me all to himself—I had been gone too much.

"That's not good, to hit Bubba," I said, but I kissed him and forgave him, and anyway, Bubba had his mother to sleep with.

I tucked myself in, Blaze next to me, and picked up a book.

I couldn't read, and it was a long time before I got to sleep.